THE
DOLLAR
COLLAR

AND OTHER STORIES

BY ED L'HEUREUX

ISBN 0-9616341-0-3

Printed in the United States of America

First Edition
1 2 3 4 5 6 7 8 9 10

Printing by McNaughton & Gunn

Consulting by Loiry Publishing House

TABLE OF CONTENTS

ACKNOWLEDGMENT

Special thanks for this book is extended to my editor, a consummate professional, Mrs. Carol Loiry of Loiry Publishing House, Tallahassee, Florida, for her steadfast belief in my work, her skillful editing of copy and her wonderful enthusiasm for the prospect of THE DOLLAR COLLAR.

This Book is Dedicated to

My wife, Laura, for understanding why I must write, to my mother, Dorothy, for all that she is, to those who are simply better because of her life, and to my friend, Dr. Alan Price, for his encouragement as I struggled with my desire to write.

THE DOLLAR COLLAR

"Grab a number and stay close in line so you can hear when I call it," coolly jawed the shop owner again. "Sorry we ain't got no more chairs. If bid'nes keeps boomin' out here on da i'land with all dem projects, I'll lease a bigger place and lay in more chairs for you folks." A carnival huckster could not have been more enticing to those standing with burning feet on the unforgiving floor.

Twenty minutes earlier, without being told, Harry had selected a plastic shiny number from the hook on the counter and found himself now, in glancing about him, only midway in numerical sequence from an audience with his excellency, Wally, the portly, curt counter barker, who doubled as shop owner and its sole repairman. Calculating a dozen and a half milling people compacted into a serpentine line in the confined customer area at the small motor repair shop, Harry assessed his relative position and ruefully gauged at least a forty-five minute, snail-pace ordeal until his summons to the counter.

Harry was good at calculating things. It was his job. He was a bright, tormented, young account executive with one of the "Big Eight" accounting firms, daily scrambling for daylight atop the heap in swarming Manhattan. Partnership overtures and all the attendant affluences that it would provide were at best only five years away, he had often ciphered, and then, with that juicy eventuality, he was certain he could relax. Surely then, he could slow down and begin to savor this pell-mell excursion commonly called life.

Protected in a brown paper bag and cradled in the crook of one jostled arm, he snugly clutched the electric mixer that was his sick patient this Saturday morning. The mixer wouldn't whirl anymore, and mutely couldn't explain where it hurt, so, on this delicious Indian summer morning, Harry, attired in khaki pants and an itchy wool shirt, was there, sardined tightly in the crowd in a cramped, huddled position identical to the press of his work week elevators and his rapid transit familiarity, save for the merciful absence of a tailored, three-piece suit.

9

Immediately before him in the fretful, swaying line, a plump, elderly lady, surrounded by a worn, brown coat much too large even for her roundness, wheezily shuffled forward, each time the line edged ahead, sliding before her on the tiled floor, a guarded shopping bag. Behind Harry, a young woman with uncombed, streaky yellow hair, punished bubble gum loudly, cracking it with abandon between bulbous lips. Periodically, she hiked a smear-faced, sleepy infant from her waist to her bosom and moaned audibly with impatience, indelicately informing everyone in their shared cell that she damned well would appreciate a chair from somewhere.

The line snaked across the front of the shop behind Harry, allowing spears of glass-bent sunlight to warm the backs of gloomy, dull-faced customers. Few in the group spoke, rather like the quietude that reigns in a building elevator, where the nearness of all threatens privacy and renders people tense and speechless. Harry had often wondered about elevators, everyone facing forward, rigid, motionless, with eyes locked on the blinking control panel, eager for their floor, anxious for their exit, sharing nothing, together yet far distant with their chosen reticence.

Two young, swarthy foreigners, perhaps brothers, were engrossed in their native tongue where the line met the front door of the shop. They gesticulated exuberantly when they spoke and the older appearing one emphatically was lecturing his wide-eyed companion. Harry understood nothing they said but surmised that the older one had been in America for some time and the other had only recently arrived. With dark eyes flashing, they reveled in their cryptic banter and enjoyed the inquisitive, uneasy stares it provoked.

Near the front of the line, a slouching, beat-tapping teenager, scabbard thin, wearing dirty jeans with an obscene T-shirt and hidden behind silver-tinted sunglasses, hoarded one of the few available chairs. He scooted it forward beneath him without rising each time Wally permitted the line to notch forward with concluded customer business at the counter. With his chair he moved along a suitcase-sized radio, which was volumed lower now in reluctant compliance to the carping demands of several customers. Even Wally had challenged him to pipe it down. Harry wished that somehow he could roust from him that smothered chair so he could offer it to the young woman with the baby.

Harry surveyed each person about him. Gloomily, he had the time to observe them. The early day outside, now russet and golden, was tantalizingly distant, its lure unreachable with its grandeur punishing the collective doleful eyes inside which peered out through window panes lined with moldings like vertical prison bars.

Along the sullen pilgrimage to the counter, two customers behind Harry, was a man with whom Harry felt he could identify. He was thirtyish, slim and balding, and he was dressed in creased khaki pants and a wool, checkered shirt only slightly different from the one Harry wore. He pouted openly with his circumstance, clicking his teeth annoyingly as he waited in line. Harry found himself chatting with him, across and over the baby-baggaged, whining mother behind him. They flung polite, confined barbs esoterically to one another as sour grapes releases of tension, above the misery of their wait.

Having to bob his head continually around her buffer between them as he tried to converse, Harry finally ushered her to a position before him in line. She obliged his open palm and managed a wan, pink-gummed smile, wishing instead that his politeness had produced a chair. He was one person further back from Wally's altar but he glowed with Samaritan warmth with his gesture, and, now, he rationalized, he was able to converse more easily with his suburban likeness.

"Twenty-three," the man stated dryly, when Harry came back next to him after escorting the young woman and her now fitfully awake and gooey armload forward one position in line.

"Twenty-three?" queried Harry, "twenty-three skidoo?" he ventured shruggingly, knowing this new acquaintance, this college-bred man, would recognize his obvious reference to

11

the flapper-era idiom of their parent's youth.

"Twenty-three lousy, little motorized machines around my Long Island monstrosity called a house that can go on the blink, ruining Saturday mornings like this one," he explained, acknowledging with a nod, familiarity with Harry's 'twenty-three skidoo' reference.

"That many, huh?"

"That many."

Harry tallied his own list at his house. Damn near twenty-three himself, he calculated privately. The arithmetic disturbed him.

"What's yours?" the man asked, gesturing toward Harry's package.

"Oh, this. Just an electric mixer. And yours?" inquired Harry, motioning his free hand toward the man's similarly wrapped object.

"Electric skillet. The clunker."

Both men spoke easily, colloquially, recognizing their mutual genre, commuter executives by trade, contented suburbanites only by vocational chance.

"And what are you giving up now to be here in this rotten line?" the man interrogated.

"I guess my hobby," Harry allowed reluctantly, after a momentary pause, "I make wood furniture; chests and chairs and things."

"You?"

"Usually have a Saturday morning golf game. What a day to be out." He jerked a thumb to the window panes behind them. The golden streaks of sun slanted in to expose the dusty, checkerboard squares beneath their feet. High clouds outside danced with miraging spots of glare in a puppet show of hide-and-seek deception across the tile floor.

"Don't tell me, let me guess," he continued. They hadn't even introduced themselves. "Your wife's got a shindig a week from tonight. People whom you don't particularly like, trooping in for snacks, drinks, and a little music, right?"

"Go on," replied Harry with rapt curiosity.

"Your mixer is needed to stir up some frilly little something, it's ailing, so you get elected today and she'll pick it up later next week while you're pounding around in Gotham City like me, chasing your dream." Again he jerked his thumb back toward the windows, in the direction of their skyscraper salt mine to the west.

"Could be," admitted Harry, now fully unmasked to the planned drudgery at his home the following Saturday night.

"Well, am I warm?"

"Yes," shrugged Harry, "more than warm, you're right on."

"Well, me too," he pined. "This skillet is needed to burn some of our hors d' oeuvres." He gestured a mock toss of his bundle out through the windows.

"I'll bet our dull parties start at the same time."

"Seven?" poked Harry timidly, almost afraid to encourage this modern day Nostradamus beside him.

His new acquaintance roared agreement, "Unreal," he blurted. "Seven, naturally. Say, let's crash each other's. Can't be less fun."

"Really," answered Harry resignedly.

Their line crept forward again, edging toward Wally. A senior citizen sagged against the counter, supported by a cane clutched in a blue-corded grasp of bones. He was warmly dressed, buttoned to his chin, but no two colors matched, even remotely. A blue-green social security check, shorn of envelope, protruded precariously from his breast pocket as a framed invitation for a street thief.

He and Wally were arguing. The old gent raised his raspy, quaking voice repeatedly. Harry could not fathom if he were mad or if deafness, cloaking his frustration, made him raise his voice.

"I need a claim check or least a name," finalized Wally gesturing impatiently with open palms. "Live in your buildin' ain't enough. Got dozens of coffee pots and you ain't sure it's a coffee pot. I ask ya, where do I start?"

The old gent creaked away from the counter smiling sheepishly. The line parted respectfully to ease his slow

13

departure, tapped by cane sensor toward the distant door. Wally called after him, "Bring me a claim check or at least a name." The old gent did not answer. He did not hear. "Honest to God, some people," remarked Wally aloud, seeking endorsement of his unbending firmness from those who remained. He received none.

"Harry Connelly," offered Harry, extending his right hand, while adjusting his packaged load in the bend of the other arm.

"Jim," blandly returned his clairvoyant new acquaintance.

"Just Jim?" questioned Harry, expecting a last name to follow.

"Right, Jim. No need for last names, we'll never see each other again."

"That's pretty cynical, isn't it?" Harry asserted.

"Jim Halloran," confessed Jim, laughingly, "I guess that was pretty cynical."

"And what do you do, Jim?" Harry pursued, winning a tactical round with this glib conversationalist.

"Commodities. Wall Street?" He drew the words out slowly, mockingly, devoid of personal pride with their significance.

"Oh!" added Harry, arching his eyebrows with a startle of interest etched across his face. "Interesting, I dare say."

"Interesting? Hardly. A pressure cooker, for damn sure."

"Do you do well...I mean...not being presumptuous or anything, I mean," Harry affirmed apologetically.

"Make a lot of money, if that's what you mean. But, so what. I'm here in this fool line with you on Saturday morning and not playing golf. What's the dif'?"

The angular teenager with his acquired folding chair shadow had reached the counter. Never far from his radio, large enough, seemingly, to be seen from a jetliner window from miles above the Sahara, he rose to talk with Wally and, for the first time, showed no further interest in his chair which he had scooted along rooted to his bottom for nearly an hour. Harry seized his opportunity and broke from the line. He bolted forward and confiscated the discarded chair. Re-

14

turning with it in tow, he offered it openly to the young mother and her baby. She squatted, heapily, gasping for breath, and grunted her thanks with a blush of appreciation surfacing through smudgy circles of orange and pink cosmetics.

"And you, Harry, what's your line?" probed Jim.

"Accounting. Midtown."

"Hm'm. Accounting. Interesting, I bet?" taunted Jim.

Harry sensed his drift and understood the verbal arrow winged his way in response to his inquiry moments earlier.

"Sometimes, after eight or ten hours in closed-door sessions with clients who can make or break your year on whim alone, it ceases to be interesting," assured Harry.

Jim howled with delight, slapping his outer thigh with a hand that had hung despondently by curled thumb in a belt loop at his waist. "You mean you've got those slate gray jowls and cold dark eyes up there in midtown too?"

"Slate gray jowls and cold dark eyes," Harry repeated lamely, inspecting each word with patient mental tweezers of dissection. "Hm'm...is that the title of a new novel"?

"Could be, at that," mused Jim with a shrug. "Hadn't thought of that. Maybe even a sitcom next season on the tube." He punished his thigh again resoundingly, elated with his self-proclaimed cleverness.

"Slate gray jowls and cold dark eyes. That's what they look like for sure," murmured Harry, almost inaudibly to himself.

Harry liked Jim. Jim made him feel uneasy and guilty, his grousing outspokenness was disarming, and it rallied him to the precipice of flaming, though uncharted, action. That was good Harry felt. Jim reminded Harry of one of those brave citizens at an annual small town meeting in New England, speaking up to rally a cause that was just and fair, regardless of unpopular consequences.

Body heat, released from the press of stuffily confined customers, radiated wavily, gradually warming the little waiting room. The sun, arching onward outside, lengthened swatches of trapezoidal glare on the linty floor. Harry loosened the top button of his wool shirt, and shook his wrists

15

after also loosening his cuff buttons. The elderly lady, imprisoned in the big, brown coat, loosened nothing. The toasting little room, shrinking with heat as the morning droned on, did not bother her. Harry concluded that her poor circulation disguised the progression of rising temperature.

A middle-aged couple, undoubtedly married, hoisted two laden shopping bags to the counter before Wally. Wally received them pompously as if the treasure trove of clattering metal they began to stack before him was not tribute enough to win his lordly favor.

"I'll take it all in, youse and da people in da buildin' but got to be in your name. Need a slip signed. Dat way, somethin' go wrong, we don't get no grief from 'dem real owners. Youse 'sponible."

The lady did all the talking. The gentleman stood by timidly, slumping away from the throng behind him, choosing not to turn to endure their collective stare, which was witheringly hot in laser-stabbing annoyance with the huge array of repairs Wally now was logging in meticulously at the counter.

"Christ, they'll be up there with that pile of junk 'til the dinosaurs return", scowled Jim. "Why didn't they come on a weekday? I would be about on number six now", he moaned, "that delicate little par three water hole." He swung an invisible golf club with one arm as best he could, confined in line and juggling his wrapped skillet, and then he cupped his free hand over his eyes as a makeshift visor in order to follow the fantasy flight of his mock swing.

"I know I'm going to hate that party next Saturday."

Harry was disconsolate too. He had been humming along at dawn, singing to himself in his garage. He wanted that lowboy finished by Christmas. It was really taking shape. The sturdy parts, once assembled, would last three hundred years in their final form. It hadn't mattered that he had labored on it periodiclly since early summer. The time spent on it hadn't seemed long at all. Harry wondered if the world would be around in three hundred years to call his lowboy a homemade antique. The thought was morbid and it distressed him, captive there in the little shop, so he wrestled with dismissing it quickly from his consciousness.

"I call it the hassle factor," Jim declared, returning Harry from the pleasure of his hobby trance to their grumpy circumstance, waiting endlessly in the shop. He continued without waiting for a reaction.

"The more you earn, the more you acquire, meaning the more that can go wrong with stuff, meaning then, the more you got to give up what you really want to do, to take time to get all the stuff fixed the lousy job let you buy in the first place."

"Tell me about commodities," interposed Harry, fighting his consummate displeasure with his fretful position in line, still fully five victims away from Wally, and unnerved further by Jim's home striking honesty and wisdom.

"C-O-M-M-O-D-I-T-I-E-S! Not much to tell, and even then you'd think me cynical," wearied Jim with lackluster in his trailing voice.

"No, really, go on," Harry urged, desperate for a change of subject.

Jim closed his eyes momentarily, forming the scene dramatically in his mind that he could showcase for Harry.

"I wear cotton in my ears on the exchange floor to save my hearing, my hand shakes when I write the orders, and I'm thirty-four years old. Succinct enough? Next subject, please!"

Harry furtively scanned the room again, without replying. There was certainly nothing else he wanted to know about commodities. Jim had that uncanny facility for inflaming indecision, disturbing complacency, and rallying people to action. He would be incorrigible holding forth with an audience at a bar rail with a drink as a shillelagh.

Only Jim and he had shared any real mutual discourse during the entire vigil in line except for the two foreigners whom Harry now quite convincingly felt were brothers. Just like in elevators were these people, those damned elevators, those vertical, mute mechanical tombs.

A black limousine thundered to a stop outside the shop and, snarling traffic, double-parked there with its engine purring powerfully. A block-shouldered man, with a sleek shaven face of black wire, emerged from the passenger side door and bent to instruct the driver. He then strode to the door of the shop, entered, and skirted the line, making a beeline for Wally's counter. He wore a black suit, accented with a thin pinstripe, and an immaculate felt homburg crowned his lacquered raven hair.

Wally had not seen him enter but when his foreboding presence darkly materialized at his counter, he dropped his tally of incoming goods from the two shopping bags and abruptly left the counter. He retreated into the belly of the shop, behind a beaded, swaying curtain and moments later the muffled whirr of a lathe sputtered to reluctant duty.

"What the Sam Hill," purpled Jim. "What's he got against lines anyhow? He got cholera?" Jim was not loudly vocal. He made his point to Harry but he did not display his displeasure audibly to others, so intimidating was the figure of the man in black.

Wally stayed fully ten minutes in the workroom. To every curious tilted ear, the unseen lathe coughed and groaned at its petulant labor. The monolithic stranger spoke to no one and deigned to engage no gaze whatsoever. He smoked two cigarettes during his wait directly beneath the red-lettered "No Smoking" placard, which was conspicuously perched with tacks above the counter and, when finished, ground the remains of both into the tile floor with a clamping press of heel. No one spoke up against him. During his stay, everyone huddled even closer, like barnyard chicks on a winter morning, and practically no conversation emitted from the assemblage. Harry wondered if this group could be meeker in the frigid yard of a concentration compound during early morning rollcall musters.

The man in black stood easily, patiently, disinterestingly oblivious to the others about him. He did not commandeer the chair from the young woman with her arm-flailing, squirmy

18

lap child although she sat close to him. Harry was relieved for that. He was not above vigilantism. He was glad he didn't have to prove it.

Wally returned with a neatly folded package secured with string and tape, and handed it across the counter. He dismissed unoffered remuneration with an obsequious bowing wave. The man, remaining aloof, turned and exited from the shop. The congested street outside sighed with relief when the invisible carbon monoxide cloud splendidly began to dissolve after the shiny black auto purred away.

Wally returned to his counter duties seemingly more pompous than before, as if real excitement in serving the ward king had been his fleeting good fortune and now he was back to his mundane routine of helping just plain, everyday people.

Jim continued to cackle, rambling about a myriad of topics, lathering his conversation with cynicism after the annoying visit from the blase' stranger in black, who had received such preferential treatment from Wally.

Dejectedly, Harry listened only half-heartedly to Jim now. He needed to listen no longer. Jim's cathartic dissertation was working steadily as a relentless laxative in Harry's mind. Jim lampooned city government, suburban government, all politicians, and garnished his Hyde Park, soap-box tirade at conclusion with a desultory report on total world forest denudation from the horrors of acid rain.

Harry knew Jim was correct in large measure, hammering away from his lofty, self-styled pulpit but it pained him to listen. Jim offered no solutions, just restatements of problems. Desperately, he tuned Jim out for order to return to his brain, but Jim's words lingered and beat within his head like the wing-whooshing rush of shrieking, hungry bats bursting from their cave entrance at dim of evening. How he missed that lowboy, emerging from nothingness, forming with promise and care, awaiting its master's return to the quiet garage.

The line, tortoise-like, crawled forward again. Harry was still three customers away from the counter, the local Lourdes for mechanical devices, that sacred shrine to the gatherer of

19

energy saving contraptions. Suddenly, from the round-shouldered, sullen queue, Harry bolted again. Jim appeared surprised and wondered for whom he was now seeking a folding chair.

An empty, metal trash can, fresh with plastic liner, stood at the front of the line, beside the counter. Harry halted before it and stood there rooted with decisiveness coursing hotly through his blood. Beading droplets glistened on his forehead. Then, in a heart-stopping, dramatic moment, suspended in time, Harry loosened his package into the dark maw of the cylinder. At first his fingers opened hesitantly, then willfully, with that prickled tingle which rushes into the brain at a momentous crossroad in life. The package fell forever, down the deep abyss, down, down, down, its passage slowed in time with the portent of its great meaning. It struck the empty bottom resoundingly with the clashing finality of orchestral cymbals.

"He's away. Away. Damn it, he's away!" cried Jim, bursting inwardly with clarity, his face incredulous. Wally looked up, startled by the sound. The elderly lady turned her head, lazily, without moving her feet and branded a mark on Harry's forehead with a disdainful leer that scolded wastefulness with his discarding action. The young woman, sagging in the chair with her bundle of baby, increased the cadence of her popping lips and stared impassively with eyes that uttered no understanding. The two foreigners ceased their gibberish and folded their arms in a cradle across their chests and awaited Harry's next performance.

Jim's mouth flew open, agape like the zinging, opening drawer of an old wooden cash register, as Harry moved quickly, unceremoniously, toward the door. He winked at Jim as he passed.

Wally called after Harry. "Watchamatta? Don't get sore, have a little patienc' will ya? Be with ya in a few minutes, buddy."

Harry paused in the doorway and answered him. "Not your fault. My fault. No more time today for that mixer." He winked again at Jim still fettered in line and exited without further fanfare.

"He's gone," murmured Jim. He cursed his own puny bravado and envied Harry's bold action. "Christ, he's made it. He's done it," babbled Jim to no audience. The person behind him nudged him in the small of his back with a rigid index finger, encouraging him to close up the line with Harry's departure. "I've seen it before, rare as it is," lashed Jim, shuffling forward to claim Harry's slot. "He's free." Jim had the second sight. Almost always each year it helped him in balancing his commodity accounts for profit in his favor.

*   *   *

On the eastern slopes in the Appalachians, in the high piedmont where gently rising foothills graduate to true mountains, a few people use electric toothbrushes. Electric toothbrushes are fine but the flouride in the still clean water there allows a satisfactory teeth cleaning chore to be accomplished by flossing and manually brushing teeth with a good dentifrice. Harry, like most people, uses a manual toothbrush there now.

Harry sells a little real estate. There isn't a great deal of real estate changing ownership on that eastern slope region but most people in real estate there are content with that circumstance. Their biggest fear is that someday there could be a galloping, brisk real estate market emerging about them. The thought rests uneasily with them.

Harry rents a cottage and leases a modest work area in a carpentry shop where he hums devotedly at his natural pace over a variety of rough-hewn pieces of furniture, in various stages of patient completion. New orders for his talent tally controllably, steadily, with the acceptance of his fine work.

The rough rash is gone from his neck where once his mandatory necktie rubbed, and the accompanying twitch in his head, caused by that garroting,. satin rope, also has disappeared.

21

It was Indian summer again in the Appalachians. The natural rouge and lipstick of autumn flirted on the slopes above Harry's little hamlet. Nearly a full year had passed since another Indian summer splendor had wafted symphonically through certain repair shop windows. Harry's unproclaimed apprenticeship for acceptance in his new town was complete. Folks there had been courteous from the day of his arrival, now they were friendly, in that hardy, rugged, solid small town way, near, reachable, accessible, but never meddlesome with their closeness.

Over Christmas vacation, short weeks after Harry's arrival the previous year, his two small children had visited, and twice again in the present year, once in the blossoming riot of spring and for a longer period in the greenness of ripe summer, they had taken the train down with delivery instructions for conductors pinned securely to her blouse and to his shirt. Each time when the moment came for their return, they squawkingly had to be practically roped to their assigned seats, so enjoyable had been their interlude with their father and his quiet town.

Harry's wife had been mortified by his abrupt metamorphosis. When he had left that previous November, he had asked her to follow. Instead, she had trooped off angrily to counsel with her mother upstate, and then, assuaged with righteous indignation there, had sought huffily the further support of her sagacious nana. Only a remnant of sympathy emanating there from the wise grande dame sent her scurrying back to her bevy of girlfriends for loyal vindication and certain justification.

In the early weeks after Harry's dash for life, those girlfriends nursed her petulant wound like syndicated columnists for the lovelorn. What a poor commuter Harry had been, they inferred, unwilling in essence to spade out daily, weekly, monthly, an early and tidy grave for himself. But then after a brisk, adamant crusade their collective guidon was stored and they returned to the more pressing tasks of arranging vapid, snobbish little dinner parties for each other, their fellow

22

prisoners, who remained behind Harry in the thick, sticky cauldron of exurbia.

Harry's wife was coming down to join him this very day. He would be glad to see her after so many months and he hoped she would stay. He had been practicing shaving daily again, having tumbled into the blissful pattern of shaving only for real estate and not for his unexamining wood furniture customers, who never noticed his stubby jowls, entranced instead by his workmanship of expert woodcrafting.

However, beyond shaving and appropriate politeness, there would be no other supplicant submission on his part, and he expected no meekness or apology from her. Harry knew something about the way of things, he knew few people were always right or always wrong about very much indeed, and that the enigmatic ways of life label us only through the eyes of other beholders, perhaps as confused as we.

Often, while singing and whistling, curling aromatic chips of knot-stained bark off knobby logs with his blockplane, Harry would think about elevators. He didn't miss elevators but he would think of them. Harry had journeyed vertical miles on elevators, storming to jolting destinations in the sky. The sepulchral quiet in them never changed. It was always there.

Harry hoped the impersonality in elevators was really conscious thoughtfulness, stilled introspection, and peaceful wonder with the complexity of life itself. But he was not convinced that the hush in elevators rose, with their ascent, to those lofty meadows of understanding. He just didn't know, he wasn't smart enough to know, but he hoped for elevators and those harried, driven souls who travel those endless shafts of silence.

PRICE AS BOTTOM LINE

By nature, human beings abhor change even when all evidence points to change as their only logical course of action. Change is difficult, unnatural, often overwhelming. Their status quo, even miserable status quo, is comfortable like the wearing of Saturday clothes and a silent, quiet telephone on that wonderful day. Reluctance to change is Newton's laboratory law of inertia in a private, personal setting. Once set in motion toward some end, humans will rationalize the steadfast pursuit of that motion to blind enslavement with it despite clear, indisputable signs which scream for needed, abrupt change.

Humans are not always lazy or indifferent with their hesitation for change. Laudably, they often demonstrate staunch pluck with it and sometimes are simply "long suffering and hope springing eternal" in the clutch of a situation, wrestling desperately with it, in the fervent hope that improvement beckons beyond the next bend, and that their painstaking efforts to make it right, to give it worth, and to carve a viable future for it will not be ground to dust, to slip, horribly, between their caring fingers, wafted away cruelly by an insensitive gust of wind.

The dreams of good people die hard. This speaks well for people. Tussle, grope, and perseverance are altogether good connectors in an ever fickle world. Aboard this crazy, spinning orb they serve as mortar, pitch, and nail and provide stability, steadiness, and, best of all, inner satisfaction for contented reflection later, on the well running of the race.

What does a person do when a business career looks bleak and barren when that person is only halfway home from that two score assessment exacted from us known as our working life sentence? What does a person do when his daily beginning each day smells like soggy coffee grounds and stale water dashed upon the hissing, mocking embers of a hurriedly doused campfire?

Get perspective, you argue! Yes, perhaps. Redouble the effort? Let's ponder that. Improve the attitude? That is always good. Examine your priorities? Fine, that's a universal chapter in all the self-improvement gospels.

*   *   *

Jonathan's campfire brain was dying, fizzing pitifully with the stench of old coffee grounds and stale water. He had to find his resolve for change. He had to force himself to remove his mid-life slippers and replace them with stiff brogans, adventure shoes that bound a little with their hiking newness. He had to experience adversity, embarrassment, unpleasantness, as a test, as a precursor to those feelings which sting a person at mid-life when circumstances dictate job change and all that attendant employment service trauma, apologizing for your present unrest, bulwarking with emphatic rhetoric your future worth to someone or something, when you never believed you would be there again, in the damning sweaty collar wet long after your shower, applying for another job, another career promise, another devotion to the dream and decree of another.

Jonathan's heart thumped fast, expectantly, that first cool April daybreak when he eased quietly away from his home, hopeful not to awaken his lovely, sleeping family. The ignition switch of his car was icily cold and the windows were befogged in mist. The slow, short drive to a neighborhood highway seemed endless, torturously stretched, like the hollow, echoing footsteps of one condemned to the gallows, with hundreds of hushed lips and staring eyes present, lining the final path.

He was frightened. But, he knew he had to start and finish his concocted experiment or perish with the unspeakable death of a coward. He knew he would be misunderstood by family and friends but he had to learn something about himself, about his will, and somehow send foolish pride packing, exiled, exorcised forever from his being.

His experiment lasted one month, eight mornings in all, Saturdays and Sundays, and when it was concluded, the prayerful rush for fulfillment was his in greater measure, with boundless clarity beyond any wild hope he ever imagined. The prize won, pennies in street value, was priceless beyond pricing, valuable beyond appraisal.

In ragged clothes, with uncombed hair tousled by restless sleep, for one month of weekends, beginning at daybreak and lasting two or three hours well into the early morning dawn, from gutter and ditch along highways near his home, Jonathan collected littered cans in garbage bags.

Beginnings are so difficult. People eschew beginnings as they do change. They delay beginnings, fear beginnings. They hate the jar and rattle and oiliness of grinding gears that signal the beginning of change of motion. Beginnings are like starchy new clothes, bought for you as a child to commemorate a holiday, clothes you wouldn't buy yourself, clothes that rub and chafe about the soft flesh with their machine-smell newness and fabric stiffness.

Jonathan purposely picked highways near his home as he knew he had to encounter, eye to eye, the surprised look of neighbors flashing by who knew him in order to learn something about his own pride. To hunt for aluminum cans twenty miles from home, falsely protected from discovery stares, disguised by his remoteness from known neighborhoods, would have been meaningless.

He selected weekend mornings because the second thrust of his experiment was to experience first hand the arduous chore of stooping to conquer cans for his plastic sack, for compensation later at the recycling scale and weekend party-goers, passing in the wee hours, would litter the shoulders of the road best on weekend nights.

His soul was naked and his body was shabbily clad. He was ready, he thought, as he parked along the dewy roadside with a two mile ribbon of road stretching before him, boasting a plump aluminum weekend harvest on either side, ripe for gathering. Was he the first to come that day? He shuddered with apprehension. With the bad economy, had not others come in the darkness before him to gather? He was fortunate. The strewn aluminum plenty was untouched that first morning.

He wasn't as ready as he thought. Totally enthused with the

expectation of his project, he began his trek with a great sense of ambivalent embarrassment. Bare solace for the humbling pursuit was comfort provided by the answer to one haunting question he had harbored privately. He was not masochistic. He had worried about that. The initial pain of this menial venture was so intense that he practically reveled in the fact that the experiment was sound and that he was sane with no masochistic cause for his chosen course.

The first morning he never looked up from his work. He stooped, collected, moved on, sloshing in the soggy earth, emptying old cans with rain water and new cans with remaining putrid libations, before plopping them with a metallic tinkle into his sack. He could not look up that day and when the morning wore on and early weekend traffic yawned about, he hated his cowardice. The agony of not knowing who saw him was worse than any real encounter. Still, bent to his work, he refused to look up, wondering that first morning if this embarrassment had been common at first to convicts on a chain gang, in a passed generation.

He walked that first morning until his parked car was only a dot on the horizon when he turned to look. Logistically he had been unschooled. He would learn fast. His plastic sack was full, slung across his shoulder in Santa fashion. He had an unproductive, grumpy walk back to his car over a canned field of plenty on the other side of the road with no place to store them. "Lout! You dumb lout," he mumbled. "Only venture out halfway, fool, with sack capacity left for the return trip. What a lousy entrepreneur you are. Don't you know the meaning of time management?"

He returned home to a still sleeping family. After storing his bounty safely in a shed behind his home, Jonathan tiptoed with morning paper to his easy chair and slumped there with weary reflection. His acid test that morning was concluded, staged before the world in his outdoor laboratory. His litmus paper, tantalizingly chameleon, had changed colors properly. The test was positive.

In full dark the following morning, he arose before the

urging toll of his alarm clock. He would be so brave that day, that Sunday, he vowed with peacockish boast. People would stay in bed on Sunday, he calculated. There wouldn't be so many out and about and he was certain that his friends in their upper middle class cocoons would sleep, so he could peek about this morning without fear of recognition. Surely, he mused, only fisherman, paper routers, and delivery trucks would be stirring.

He drove to another area close to his home. When he cut the engine, however, the confidence exuded earlier, prodded and braced with morning coffee, vanished. He was frightened again. The familiar road was now foreign to him. He longed for the road of yesterday as he knew something of its feel and touch. The sound of cars passing as he worked was maddening. In the still of early morning he dreaded their faint approach, which grew louder, then deafeningly louder, forever dissonant as they drew near to his hunched form. Closer and closer they came and then mercifully, with a whoosh they would pass and be gone. He wallowed in shame and would not look to engage the eye of any passing motorist.

Anxiously, Jonathan passed the next five days awash in personal disappointment with his reluctance to be identified. He steeled himself with a resolve that week to plunge, to absorb, to venture, to disarm his shame the following Saturday morning. And, he did.

When he first looked up from the ditch early that second Saturday, with ready, rehearsed disclaimer, eager to blurt aloud to any acquaintance that he was only experimenting, that he still had a job, that he didn't need to be there, that he was somebody, nothing at all needed to be defended, as the motorist was a stranger, and, to his gaping astonishment, the motorist never even looked Jonathan's way even though he was as conspicuous as a whale in a bathtub.

The fear of the unknown was classic in its shocking irony. The motorist had not looked in his direction. Hundreds of divergent reasons raced through Jonathan's searching mind. And then in cool, calming analysis, as he stood dumbly, comically beside his green plastic sack, the most logical answer was provided miraculously to him. Could it be the motorist had his own problems with which he was engrossed as he drove and could it be that people scrounging for cans on roadsides were no longer, rare spectacles?

On the Sunday morning, his fourth day, with his ostrich-like shyness slowly and painfully being exposed to the light of the real day as he forced himself to walk and work upright, not ostentatiously, never with a hail or wave to motorists but nevertheless, no longer shunning his obvious presence either, that inevitable, dreaded first encounter occurred. He had been seen. He was naked in spirit, disrobed from dignity.

A college chum who lived near Jonathan, with whom he had enjoyed a casual but friendly association for twenty years, had surely spotted him, as he had seemed to look squarely in his direction when he had zoomed past him. Jonathan was crushed. The framework of courage gingerly forged in four harrowing days separated as weakly as cardboard sodden with rain.

The remainder of his trek that morning was anticlimactic, its conclusion hastened only to find Jonathan home in his quiet stillness much too early to phone his college chum in order to defend and explain his silly presence on the shoulder of that road. Nervously, he gulped coffee, devouring the early arriving newspaper with darting, vacuous snatches of troubled unrest. The hands on the wallclock appeared rooted, unmoving, agonizingly halted at an hour too early to call. Finally, at nearly nine o'clock, hardly a decorous hour to dial even a close friend on a Sunday morning, after the passing of an eternity in which his shame and guilt was transmogrified to flights of fiendish illusion, he called.

"Be home again! Be home," muttered Jonathan into the mouthpiece. Ring! Ring! Ring! "Be home," whined Jonathan. A cautious voice answered.

"I...I am trying something! I...I don't have to pick up cans," blurted Jonathan in a torrent of placated defense, after scarcely introducing himself.

32

"It's an experiment, that's all it is. Really, only that."

"Whatever do you mean?" replied his perplexed college chum.

"I...I mean me, by...by the road this morning. I still have a good job and all."

"What road?" he inquired annoyingly.

"Where you saw me with the cans," offered Jonathan.

"I didn't see you anywhere. What is this all about? I only remember being on that road."

"Oh!" Jonathan answered hollowly, with consummate embarrassment.

"You...you didn't see me there?"

"No!"

Jonathan went on to explain as best he might but nothing came out right. He was pedantic, then esoteric, and finally he tried to salvage it with a little gossip from their past but the phone call, doomed from its inception, sputtered and then died with ignominy.

He had not been seen. How foolish he felt. Wildly imagining the whole confrontation, conjuring its first terror in his mind long before he began the project, he had been certain it had occurred. But he had been mistaken. So poised had he been for this offending, rude stigma that he had stumbled headlong into the abyss of an erroneous conclusion.

As the month progressed, he began to study his experiment empirically. He assembled mind notes. By the third weekend, he was being seen by hundreds of early motorists as he was staying out longer, filling a second and even a third plastic sack. He trudged miles on roads leading out like spokes of a wheel from the refuge of his home. The gathering treasure trove of sacked cans piled up in his utility shed.

Television commercials, strategically barked decibels higher than normal viewing, for the sake of consumer attention, fell on his deaf ears. He knew which beers sold best and which soft drinks were favored. His early morning rounds, miles of stooping and sorting, were exact enough for drawn conclusions in consumer preference that would have

33

rivaled the Madison Avenue advertising ratings. The choice people preferred in drinking, in smoking, in chewing, in snacking, in safely fornicating, lay strewn before him in varying degrees of residuary, spent usage as clear as a Rand McNally road map.

The strangest phenomena of all for Jonathan as he walked was the people whisking by, piloting all manner of conveyance. Broad, general conclusions about their comfort or discomfort with his presence began to emerge. He catalogued data mentally as he went, fighting for objectivity without a clinical notebook in which to record his impressions. He wrestled with this unfolding panorama of eye contact, this succulent banquet in human reaction, wanting desperately to interpret it properly.

Toward the end of the month, Jonathan's purpose became chiefly twofold with the future profit derived from selling his cans for recycling, ancillary now to his new styled goals. First, he wanted to study what patterns he could learn from the litter habit itself and secondly, he now wanted to catalog honestly the reactions of people, seeing a slovenly dressed man grubbing for cans at break of day. However, his overriding real reason, surrounding his two lesser themes, remained inviolate, chiseled in his mind clearly as that desperate need to suffer for strength anew through valiant, uncomfortable, unknown experiences regardless of pain, with the trauma of a needed career change sweetly calling him as the bewitching Sirens to Ulysses.

Thusly, Jonathan explored a new world of experience. In the main, people in long, shiny grand cars ignored him. When he could view their reaction, as often tinted glass rendered them faceless, opaque forms, they viewed him with snobbish disdain if they condescended to glance his way at all. However, at the other extreme of the economic spectrum, people in older vehicles, broken, clanking pickup trucks, and rusty clunkers, coughing black exhaust, often grinned and even occasionally waved a greeting to him as if to say they knew his honest effort first hand, with perhaps a friend or a relative presently collecting cans on some other lonely road.

But the most interesting reaction of all for Jonathan was from that broad band of upper middle class motorists, that clawing "upward mobility", nouveau riche segment, madly living hand-to-mouth, barely abreast of their installment plan affluence, scurrying to own and achieve, chasing elusive dreams they never really defined. These people were uncomfortable when they saw him as if his presence triggered a single grain of worry about their own life, as if that unnecessary boat payment at home, that crunch to live as devout, "strungout financially afflicted" Americans pinched and pinched hard, as if they pondered momentarily, sickeningly, as they passed Jonathan the haunting notion of what was in his past that put him to collecting cans and would they ever have a similar circumstance, a seemingly cornered demand to act as he.

Always, Jonathan had risen early, often well before dawn to dabble joyfully with oils upon his easel, or to clean up a satchel of insipid paperwork dragged home from the office. Therefore, he had hoped that at his home his strange early wanderings that April would go unnoticed, homogenized as normal routine. However, he had prepared himself for the possibility of being discovered. If he were uncovered, he had vowed privately that he wold own up and explain his motives.

One day late in the month, Jonathan's son inadvertently discovered the sacks of cans stashed supposedly in hiding within the shed cache. The unspoken question mark which hooked down, hung from his furrowed brow, disturbed Jonathan. Thinking he could explain everything to such a bright young man, he had rehearsed his staged explantion for such a moment. But the words did not form as planned, his was a blank scroll, a yellowing, clean sheet of paper flapping in a typewriter.

Instead, he shouldered him close with his arm and said to him.

"Trust me, adults do strange things sometimes, son, that youths like you will only understand later. There is money for your college, don't worry. What I'm doing here is too involved to explain to you now."

35

His son accepted the sketchy dissertation and his acceptance spoke well for their relationship. Jonathan was proud. He had always been totally honest with him and now when elaboration should not be, his son had understood. Something profoundly right had been accomplished with him over the years and that knowledge warmed him.

Like a trapper sledding pelts for a snowshoe run to the trading post or a pioneer hitching his wagon for a Saturday pilgrimage to the only general store, the day arrived for Jonathan to load his goods for market. Sixteen, green plastic bags were stuffed into his car. Wearing the unwashed, sun-ripened old clothes which had served him warm during the eight cool mornings of his April discovery month, he set off for the seven mile trip to the recycling location barely able to peek through his rear view mirror with clank, stench, and clutter his untalkative companions. Many times before at the busy intersection, he had noticed the chain-linked cage on a cart which served as a mobile aluminum recycling depot, but prior to this late April morning, he had never envisioned himself as a customer with such a bounty to barter.

Sporting a shiny girlie magazine on his lap, the proprietor was slouched in a jaded, bent chaise lounge, which was laced with precarious, torn strips of vinyl webbing, groaning with dry rot. Nearby, the two front doors of an ancient Chevrolet Impala wearily hinged open to facilitate the bombardment of hard rock music upon willing and unwilling listeners over a full city block area. As scruffy as Jonathan appeared, attired in his gutter and ditch raiment, the proprietor looked worse. Jonathan's ripe old clothes could have been his Sunday best, that is, if the proprietor ever really separated Sunday from the other six days and knew about Sunday clothes.

Without a word of greeting, the proprietor attacked his sixteen plastic sacks like a starving hyena finding an unattended lion kill in the middle of the dry season. The bags were rent open with taloned, swift hands and before Jonathan could catch his breath from unloading, his cans were being madly separated into two conical piles with machine-like rapidity and indifference.

"Hey!" complained Jonathan, "Easy does it, a lot of work went into all this."

"Steel don't wash, cap'n," the attendant announced dryly without looking up, "Only 'luminum count."

"Oh!" Jonathan replied meekly after a pause, realizing he had bent and fetched eight mornings for a month, picking up cans, all cans, when really much of his treasure was worthless, unfit candidates for compensation. This bitter fact alone, notwithstanding his private war on the project with eye contact comfortableness, was enough to dampen the hardiest of spirits.

The mountain of discarded steel cans rose and proliferated. He looked away too soured to further punish himself. His eye spied a lurching derelict from a nearby tavern, tottering against a concrete lightpost, urinating in broad daylight, to a mocking cacophony of passing car horns. He turned back to his own drama, thinking it now not so bad. As much as he had always detested the salving triteness of those four taunting words, he knew that "all things are relative" was wisdom indeed.

His money cans, those chiropractic darlings, were dumped rudely with spillage into a battered rubber drum, which was slung with a grunt up to a gasping weight hook. Twice this procedure was repeated. Jonathan glowed inwardly, satisfied that he had collected, at the very least, enough of the right stuff to fill two drums.

In a flashing moment the attendant was finished. All that work and over so soon grimaced Jonathan with empty finality. A grimy carpenter apron, circled and cinched about his waist, served as business cash register. The attendant drew out from one side, stitched apart from the change section, four single dollar bills. They were different shades of green, crumpled and folded. His dirty, ugly hand, with curves of black beneath each nail, scooped down into the other section and played a moment with the change, which, when stirred in the air, gave off that odious, metallic stink identifiable as greasy, moist coinage. A quarter, a dime, and two pennies, adroitly dispensed with one hand, joined his four dollars. He had been paid. The attendant returned to his lounge chair from whence he had sauntered, without a good-bye, without a word. The business had been transacted. $4.37 was his to keep.

As Jonathan slowly drove home with beeping cars piloted by irate, neck-craning motorists impatiently passing to his left, he experienced one of the warmest rushes of satisfaction he had ever experienced in his life. He had conquered fear, shame, doubt and in his madcap rush to find himself that month with career pressures dogging his staggered step, he had run headlong into himself, and it was good, profoundly good.

With little exception, he knew that poignant morning that he never would be quite the same person again. He would not shirk responsibility, or detour from dutiful necessity. He would provide for loved ones and not make his private zest the crutch or bandage of another, but, marvelously, he knew, discovered in awareness from that month, that there was a part of him, an infinitesimal, miniscule atomic dot, long latent, but now drilled to the ready, that no one human or thing would ever totally control again.

No job, no dogma, no ideology, no sport, no child, no wife, no parent, no friend, no boss would ever own all of him again. There was a speck of him that would remain his forever, impervious as diamond to the establishment shatter, stalwart and defiant against all incursions of mental enslavement by the three-piece suit wonders of the world.

He knew through his glorious aluminum cans that whatever happened he could do again the harsh truck work of his youth, live alone in a hut bereft of friends, grind a lathe, swing a shovel, punch a register because whatever he had to do to earn a living did not matter. What mattered was what he did with his talent for himself.

For the majority of his life span, Jonathan had served others, now for that remaining smaller portion, he would serve himself, and in so doing, indirectly, only as a natural by-product from his desperate selfness, would he serve others.

38

Other things too, wonderful, elusive gifts, cherished now with their fresh, beloved capture finally were his as he slowly continued home, bathed in exultant, cold perspiration, startled to tingling understanding with his joy of clarity. His protracted adolescence was over. It had taken well into mid-life for this folly to be discarded, and now it was shrugged aside for good. He had matured. The petty need to be liked by everyone, the dismal falseness of needing to be the cynosure with every group was no longer important. He had slithered out and away, free at last, his former scaly skin already beginning to rot in the newly found sunlight.

And whether the world ever decided to decorate him greatly did not matter either. He knew he could be good, very good, and what mattered was that he was willing to pay any personal, legitimate price to fan that blazing fire within him.

He would make no apology ever again for his working life as he knew more than they. He had one thing they did not have. He had a brush, a canvas, an easel, and ideas crowned with an insatiable desire for fulfillment and only disease or death would every wrench them from his hands and mind.

Blessed $4.37.   Priceless $4.37.   Precious $4.37.

LATE SUMMER'S BRIEF SPRING

Surprisingly, a parking space was vacant today where before one never had been available. Ted had played his hometown, public golf course scores of times, earlier throughout his high school golf team days, but a space to park so ideally close to the clubhouse had not beckoned before. Nevertheless, there it was today, enticing and alluring, seemingly reserved for him, solitary between handicapped parking and the resident pro's spot, alone, amid a sea of parked cars.

As Ted parked, the day felt so strangely different to him. He really expected the gift of the parking space to be bequeathed any moment to someone more important than he. Usually, a nice, warm day in early Spring would be reason enough to be excited about a round of golf. But today somehow was special, more anticipatory, charged with electric prickle, as if something monumental were about to happen.

This morning, his favorite breakfast, waffles with strawberry jam, had been prepared especially for him and additionally, Ted's mother, the evening before had rummaged about and had found an old family relic, his striped golf shirt that he had worn superstitiously for good luck in high school on those special match days.

She had been a good listener, bless her heart. He had really opened up to her with the moody drive down from State College loosening his tongue. Although alone, they had spoken last night, in almost hushed tones, in that tender, mellifluous way in which a middle-aged widow and an only son confide, as friends with understanding overlapping within the same generation, beyond the unspoken respect of their parent and child relationship.

"They thought it was a direct result of seminary, Mom, and my decision to start next Fall, but it wasn't really," Ted pleaded. "The ribbing I got. My idea of spring break just isn't staggering around beach towns in pajamas at night, sloshing vodka out of a paper cup."

"I know, Ted," she replied understandingly, clasping her hands devotedly upon her lap. "You are well liked on the golf team and up there at school. Maybe they were just testing you," she continued reassuringly. "As your decision to become a minister with your golf talent seems, well perhaps, somewhat incongruous to them. And of course, dear, they may have been trying to justify a rowdy spring break in their own minds."

"'Catch some rays, Ted! Chase some skirts, Ted!' They were relentless. 'Come on,' they said, 'you date here on campus. Let's meet some new girls. We've got a break from matches this week, and you aren't even going with us. Square!' All week, Mom," Ted pined for sympathy. "Incessant!! And then, last night came the crowning blow. They had my Bible propped open and perched near the ceiling in my room atop a stack of pillows borrowed from every dorm room on our floor. That's when I called you, said I had had it, and asked you to get Jimmy Eckland to find us a tee time because I was coming home on break."

"You'll relax around Jimmy," comforted Ted's mother. "He knows about seminary. I told him when we spoke. He likes you and always looked up to you in high school. And one other thing, young man," she preached waggishly.

"What's that?" ventured Ted flatly.

"Don't be too put out with your friends at school. It's when people stop talking about you that you have to start worrying."

The golf course was crowded as the morning was perfect for golf. The air had that faint hint of stern May humidity, arriving now in April, a month early, with that unshakable warning of how searing the relentless Florida summers can be, when they abruptly choose to return each year to extract their seemingly endless and torturous tribute.

Jimmy met Ted on the practice tee. He had hit a bucket of balls and had assumed already that rumpled look of humorous disarray that Jimmy usually wore once he was doing what he loved doing most, playing golf with a vengeance, oblivious to everything else about him. His stripes and plaids, loosely incompatible with a clash of kaleidoscopic color, were easily one size too large for his thin, angular body. His clothes never matched but no one noticed or even cared anymore that Jimmy wasn't sartorially correct when he played golf. He was colorful enough despite his attire and wore just fine as a playing companion. His light, easy banter on golf, girls, and gossip was never a threat to anything that anyone held dear.

On the first tee, as their round of golf began, the same strange sensation Ted had experienced earlier finding his own special parking place returned. Everything seemed so clear, like that first prismatic instant when the sun pops out again after a brief summer shower. He seemed in complete charge of everything. It was eerie! The club Ted held on the first tee was an indivisible extension of his own arm. He felt he could spout poetry, recite verse, deliver a speech flawlessly.

Ted shut his eyes. The feeling one receives soon after alcohol is first tasted swept through him. Ted had sampled his share of beers during his four years at State College, most of them, admittedly, before his seminary decision, but nevertheless, he could recall that evanescent moment when the world is so orderly and tidy, when the alcohol invades as stimulant before it erupts in actuality as the insidious, anchor-dragging depressant it truly is.

In that short expanse of time, one is eloquent, omniscient, a world problem solver. It doesn't last long, that detailed, panoramic correctness. Ted recalled his anger and disappointment at those elusive moments, as perfect clarity became gossamer and then vanished altogether, not to return until that next stolen time, early on, when you drank alcohol again and that brief, warm order of all things flashed by in perfect but temporary focus.

His birdie on the first hole was routine if birdies should ever be described as commonplace. The approach shot drew to the flag as if leprechauns had labored mischievously during the night to place a gigantic magnet under the surface of the green. Scoring on holes two and three also robbed par by a shot. Their round was early, but vaguely Ted became aware of the

45

extra carry of his shots from the tees and fairways. Familiar landmarks, a tree here or a bush there, close to where second and third shots had bounced to rest customarily, were left well behind more distant points, where today he addressed those fairway shots. Jimmy noticed this too, and remarked, "You're on a real run, Ted. Maybe coming home agrees with you."

On the fourth green, Ted sighed philosophically, thinking his birdie barrage was over. He faced a nasty, undulating putt, half the length of a house. However, the nudge of the blade was perfect and it dropped for him, eons later, after a tantalizing excursion of varying speeds over its uneven path.

Ted's next drive on the long par five heart-stoppingly hugged the right dogleg out-of-bounds marker the length of its prodigious flight and died begrudgingly farther than he had ever struck a tee shot before in his life. Two standard putts followed an equally Herculean fairway wood and the five hole total tallied to a handful of birdies.

The glare of the sun, fully in their faces, on hole number six reduced the calculation of the pin placement to mirage-like uncertainty. The more they squinted at the elevated green, wavily shimmering in the late morning brightness, the more they turned away with spots dancing before their eyes. Blinded and unsure, Ted swung hurriedly. A twosome ahead, waiting in their cart at the adjoining next tee, traced the path of his shot for them when they pulled up alongside, unable at first, to locate the ball.

"You flew the green and hit the base of that pine on the roll", offered the driver. "That's you back by the pin on the ricochet."

"Bet you looked everywhere else coming up," added his companion with a touch of jealous sarcasm.

Jimmy had been his ebullient self during play on the early holes, but now his face was pale, twisted in perplexity and disbelief. Another birdie, courtesy of a convenient pine tree, silently spoke his expression. He had been playing well, not nearly as well as Ted, but his score was excellent too, fashioned in desperation by the murderous assault of the course by his astonishing companion.

46

After Ted's sixth consecutive birdie, Jimmy launched into one of his mimicking impression acts that formerly entertained and amused back in the high school classrooms. This had been Jimmy's way of easing tension around school work he never really enjoyed. He didn't know what to do or say directly with Ted's fantastic play, like avoiding, inconspicuous baseball dugout mates when their pitcher is working on a no-hit game, so he resorted to his cutup capers to remove the wonder of the match from consciousness. Ted appreciated his attempt to relax him and privately too, he hoped that normal good play would continue, but not at this uncanny, unsettling, and extraordinary pace.

His plea for just solid normalcy passed unanswered as his systematic demolition of par golf continued. Everything worked. Score card birdies were posted again on the following two holes. The majestic accuracy of his approach iron on the ninth hole drew a hollow, polite response from Jimmy.

"You want to grab a sandwich at the turn?" he offered almost apologetically, in a timid voice, scratchily higher than normal.

"No," Ted deadpanned, "let's keep going and end this thing."

Jimmy was relieved that Ted had made direct reference to his play, thereby excusing him from the topical delicacy of the occasion.

On the tenth hole, it happened. Condescendingly, Ted managed only par when his putt slid breathlessly past the cup, lipping it gently with its last gasp of roll. Jimmy let out a war whoop, and momentarily forgetting golf etiquette, pranced across the green with the high-stepping, trampling dance of an Indian rainmaker.

"Welcome back to planet Earth," he chortled. "You ain't no spaceman after all, Ted."

Jimmy popped another beer from his private, iced cache which was stowed safely aboard their cart. He had averaged a beer on each of the first three holes, his treat he had defended on his day off, playing golf not working, but he had declined

47

further indulgence until now. For several holes, Ted's miraculous performance had shocked him into a state of somber sobriety. Now, he had concluded, with Ted's mortal par, he could enjoy himself again as his companion had rejoined the human race.

The cuppy hand gaze to the flag from the next fairway was chimerical. He looked again. And a third time, rotating his head slowly, troubled and disbelieving, Ted blinked, expecting the image to fade from view. Only a modest iron shot remained there on the fairway as his third stroke to this long, par five hole. The cup was as big as a washtub. It was cavernous. Frenzied lemmings, a hundred abreast, could have easily tumbled into it. Before he took his stance, he knew an eagle was inevitable. The soothing par for Jimmy on the previous hole would be inflamed below par once again.

Jimmy drifted away, quietly hostile. Moaning and groaning indistinct incantations and gesticulating madly about in abject resignation with his bird-like arms flapping wildly, he divided his time between stumbling over unseen clumps of grass and clumsily banging the cart each time he slumped aboard.

"Should I chip it or putt here from the fringe, Jimmy?" pleaded Ted, practically begging for advice on the last hole in a puny attempt to encourage him to salvage some gratification from the torturous day.

Ted felt sorry for him. They had begun happy and carefree, hopeful to punctuate a warm, clear day with only reminiscent, old memories, and a few beers for Jimmy. Instead, unwittingly, easygoing Jimmy had become party to a round of golf that he would never see again or ever hope to duplicate himself.

"It don't matter," Jimmy measured retiringly, "it's going in the damn hole either way."

The confluence of tees and greens on the compactly routed back nine had drawn them repeatedly close to the twosome ahead who earlier had reported the pine tree, ricocheted shot. Periodically, in exchanging greetings, they had overheard those two remark, "I've seen four birdies myself," and "he has been under par every time I've looked." Later, Ted realized that this advance party had scouted word ahead at the clubhouse. When he and Jimmy arrived there at the end of play, a milling throng awaited them.

Jimmy trailed after Ted, slinking along stoop-shouldered, like a wet puppy, cold from the rain. Ted hastily wove his way through the stand of curious, questioning golfers. There was no clamor, only a low buzz of nervous unsettledness. Room to walk parted as he proceeded. It was awkward being treated like a potentate, not knowing whether his path was given freely with utter plebeian awe or only smugly, with reluctant, jealous contempt.

"Can't count it, if it happened, 'less you record it," admonished the nonchalant pro as Ted passed, with an accusatory, suspicious barb thrown above the humming murmur of the assembled group. Ted didn't respond. His exit was swift.

"These clubs are yours, Jimmy. Pick them up at the house this summer. I'll tell Mom. I'll be working away after school is out and seminary starts in the Fall. I won't have a chance to play then. Don't say anything noble now, I'm not in the mood. Just use them. I want you to have them."

They both stood in the parking lot for a moment but further words did not come. Jimmy freed the smoking driver from its liner in the golf bag and held it gingerly, as one sneakingly handles an artifact in a museum ever wary of the disapproving, eagle eyes of lounging security guards. Ted expected him to brandish it about madly in some mock swing embellished with a cute commentary, but he held it quietly, almost reverently, observing it closely up and down the shaft, as if he awaited its transformation into some magical wand.

Ted's mind whirled and his chest pounded as he drove from the golf course. Droplets of perspiration slid off his nose, pooling in succession on his lap. Mental weariness and exhilaration emoted alternately as he frightfully tried to assess the wonder of the morning. Eighteen under par! A round of fifty-four!

Overcome with bewilderment, he shivered, and clenched the steering wheel tightly as he drove, consciously grappling with the necessity of driving slowly, less his altered state of amazed preoccupation be dangerous in highway traffic.

Ted murmured to himself. "Was it Casper or Snead who carded an official fifty-nine in tournament play?" he sorted privately with racing mind. "One of them it was, I...I...I believe, I...I...I once remember reading..." he mumbled aloud to his non-existent passengers.

*   *   *

Sundays aren't the only busy days in the ministry. For him, like most ministers, Sundays were the most demanding days quite naturally, but Wednesdays too, for instance, always had been full, complete days. For twenty years, Wednesdays had been reserved as sermon writing day. The writing preparation often arranges with difficulty when one cares about sermons and, thusly for him, Wednesdays often had been painstakingly arduous as he had cared greatly about his sermons.

However, Sundays, for a minister without an associate pastor, with a fair-sized congregation to serve, stood apart in the energy consumption category. In his church, for years, that day had included a morning worship service, an afternoon study circle, an early evening youth counseling session around the dinner hour, and finally, a concluding evening prayer meeting.

Tolerantly, late each Sunday afternoon he had provided a needed respite for himself, for only an hour, at that time before youth counseling began. During that private time, his batteries were recharged and his enthusiasm rekindled for the remainder of the day. His alone time, as he had come to refer to it, had become essential. Briefly then, he immersed himself in his spa-for-the-mind interlude. Many ministers utilize similar solitary moments knowing parishioners want them alert, responsive, and dynamic in order to orchestrate for them their own unuttered, subconscious need for weekly battery recharging.

His favorite elixir during those late Sunday afternoons had become watching the professional golf tour on television. Ensconced in his study, alone, drooped in a soft chair, with no appointments during that hour, he had grown to relish this invigorating, stolen separation from the pressing reality and gravity of his work.

What a splash of color they parade about. Canary, chartreuse, magenta, mauve! And, they all dress so resplendently. Silhouetted against the contrasting lushness of the green grass, their chromatic brilliance is even more pronounced. "Do the networks have some new fancy lens device which intensifies the color of grass?" he pondered. "I bet they do, they are so clever nowadays," he speculated audibly in his private study. There was no one with him to comment on his questioning.

"I've never seen grass that green, even after a summer shower," he whispered with childlike enchantment. "And their two-toned, snappy shoes, they always appear so neat, never scuffed or dirty. I wonder what would happen if I showed up in the pulpit one Sunday morning in a bell-sleeved sweater and a pastel pullover shirt," he daydreamed prankishly. Clicking his teeth and wagging an index finger, he dismissed the thought with alacrity, fearing the idea might linger and germinate.

Applause! Polite applause is conferred on almost every shot. Applause on great shot making is understandable but it seems recognition abounds expectantly for all the players. Wouldn't it be embarrassing to be applauded in church, he fantasized. His face reddened. Thurber's Walter Mitty had nothing on him. He was living vicariously in the seclusion of his study. Well, at least occasionally when you did something particularly good and uplifting, it might be fun to hear a little applause. He sulkily embraced the playful notion for a stolen moment. Then, he shook himself with reality as quivering birds repel water from their wings before extending them into the warmth of the sunlight.

Oh, stop it, stupid! Remember the letter you received a few

years back from Mrs. Collins, reporting on her son's great success in the armed forces, and she thanking you for laying the groundwork for that success? See! That's a kind of applause, certainly, although you can't really touch it, or rather, uh, really hear it.

"The prize money offered for these tournaments is truly amazing," he fairly shouted aloud from his deep chair before muzzling the embarrassment of his unilateral conversation. His mind became mouth again, "This commentator here is telling the viewing public that the winner, for four days work, will earn enough for a new roof on the youth building, enough for a better Sunday school bus, enough for needed furniture in the nursery, to say nothing of carpet and paint for the sanctuary, and still there would be enough left for the finance committee to reconsider and finally approve my long overdue request for a salary increase. Surely," he rationalized, "that prize money isn't all profit for them! Their travel, their clothing, saints alive that clothing, their standard of living must make considerable inroads into this kind of generous remuneration," he comforted, assuaging his ruffled feathers on the matter of money and feeling better for it.

It was that time again. The late Sunday afternoons pass so quickly. "Who is it tonight?" he tried to recall, thumbing through his dilapidated appointment book, as he slid up and forward again in his chair, after switching off the television with a faint, recumbent sigh. Duty calls. He chided his mild reluctance to duty. He liked his work but he often felt inadequate and ineffective. All the correct answers simply weren't his to give every time.

"The Thompson boy" his secretary had noted beside the date in his appointment book. I don't know him at all and scarcely know his mother, he lamented as he scanned her notes for shreds of assistance with their first encounter meeting now only minutes away. She's a widow, I remember that. She seems to be coping nicely from all outside appearances I've noticed. His secretary had penciled in the margin, "'Won't study much, only lives and breathes golf,' says his mother." He

52

smiled to himself and announced privately that he liked this Thompson boy already.

Some kind of an ice-breaker would be nice though, since I don't know him. The first few minutes spent with a youth can be critical to any successful result. At that outset, in the sparring, early going, like an important job interview, youths can be alienated forever or put at ease and made to feel open and responsive. Reflecting serious again, he tallied his preparation. A twinge of nervous doubt surfaced in the form of light perspiration. He drew a finger the width of his upper lip and then afterward compressed there with a blotting hankerchief. Lately, he seemed to be having a little more difficulty in reaching these youths. Perhaps it was his age. Now, at forty-five, the unmistakable arrival of early middle age could be reminding these kids, with indelible certainty, that he was truly a full generation removed from them.

He had made some changes recently in his approach to counseling and he was particularly proud of his decision to relocate the forum of his work, from the homey atmosphere of his study to the early evening privacy of the sanctuary itself. More attention, more credence was achieved there. In the formal stillness of the sanctuary with its imposing high, vaulted ceiling and its sunset array of brilliant light, slicing through the stained glass windows, his words quietly echoed with more convincing thrust and persuasion.

He had realized a few years earlier that his study reminded these youths of their own living rooms, family rooms, or their own fathers' studies, and that, he, in that mental setting, reminded them of their own fathers, often pontificating and dictating wisdom unswervingly, upon recapturing unbending views of their own youth, through their distorted recollections of it and then subjugating advice for law as they alone perceived and codified it.

Rising slowly from his spongy chair, the tired metal coils squeaked relievably, almost disguising the humorous cracking of his slow-to-awaken ankle and knee joints. A harbinger of early arthritis had settled in, with now at middle age, no

53

immediate hindrance beyond slight annoyance. Subconsciously, he orderly brushed the lapels of his well recognizable, outfashioned brown suit. He hooked the toe of each shoe behind the opposite pant leg and rubbed himself a free shoeshine, a habit his wife decidedly loathed. He had surrendered gracefully to her protestations over the years, and in deference to her wish, he had agreed to shine his shoes this way only in private.

Leaving his study, he made his way resoundingly along the deserted concrete corridor to the sanctuary. The light clop of his shoes, bouncing within the confining walls of the archway, reverberated loudly. The oblique, yawning rays of the late afternoon sun glinted against the sheen of his worn brown suit and through his thinning shock of matching hair. No one saw him pass. He was thankful to be undisturbed this evening as he was preoccupied with his encounter session. Well-meaning parishioners usually stopped him everywhere when he was spied on the grounds and, bless their hearts, invariably, they asked the most nonsensical, inane questions. Why must he always be expected to have all the right answers?

Mrs. Thompson sat erect against the center aisle on a rear pew, her lips were pursed, strong and egalitarian, yet kind and forgiving despite their resoluteness. She was tastefully and plainly dressed and her hair, matronly arranged, was sprinkled naturally with specks of salt and pepper coloration.

With hair still matted wet in places from a recent shower, her gangling son lounged fretfully, somewhat away from her on the same pew with a downcast look of foreboding, as if any moment he expected a bailiff to emerge and lead a returning, grim jury to the unfamiliar choir loft. His shirt was unbuttoned at the throat and he had flunked tie-tying class as his Windsor knot screamed a patrician ouch!

"I want to help him if I can," Theodore mused again, reaching for the bulbous, brass knob on the heavy sanctuary door. "He's a total stranger. How can I reach him? I need some introduction, an ice-breaker." Theodore fisted the air emphatically with his other hand just before entering.

A spark of clarity ignited in his groping mind. "Eureka! Hey, I wonder if he ever shot a fifty-four," he exclaimed almost aloud, as the door creaked ponderously open. He shouted within himself with brimming exuberance. "He's a golfer. He can relate to that."

No one has ever shot a fifty-four of course, he scoffed inwardly as he extended his warm, purposeful hand to mother and then to son. It's impossible. But, he had pictured just how it could happen. Many times, dozing on momentary sabbatical leave, deep down in his armchair, he had witnessed its incredible glory, its fanciful magic, its explosive, free, fantastical gust from the window of tedium. He had been there on Sunday afternoons drifting, day-dreaming, with his eyes closed, reliving just how it could happen, just how it would be.

Perhaps he could win over this Thompson boy. He would try.

PASSING AT THE BEACH

Strolling slowly, holding hands, they approached him. She, barefoot, gathered in two bulky sweaters embattled against a stiff March ocean breeze, and he, in canvas shoes skillfully scissored open, high at the sides to let his bunions breathe, located him sitting there again, facing the spent bluster of ebb tide, which played feebly about his toes, with only foamy tribute to offer at the cease of its mighty voyage.

They always looked for him, throned in his rusty, vinyl-webbed, folding chair, as soon as they were close enough on their daily, late morning walks, to focus their two pair of septuagenarian eyes cloudily upon him.

He was there on all weekends, faceless in the throng, when the sand trembled under the crush of blaring beach buggies, and he was there on some weekdays when the sand sighed, shorn somewhat of its yoke of people, when shuffling old men in ancient swim trunks and sagging argyle socks strung on prune-wrinkled legs searched for coinage with nodding metal detectors, and plump police cruised pompously, burning city air-conditioning through open windows, with their ticketing blue lights muted, a weekday reprieval for slight speeders until the weekend beetling swarm again begged for their strict disciplinary presence.

In the boil of summer he came, when sunspots shimmered dizzily and streams of suntan lotion dripped down smeared bodies like riveting slicks of lava. He came in the numbness of January when his presence was conspicuous by its insularity, and he sat then for hours, while hungry seagulls, white as winter, squawked annoyance before scanty pickings and shore-darting birds worked diligently stealing a meal, an empty belly calendar turn from the generous pantry of summer.

His position on the beach never changed. The little staked duchy of sand could have boxed a compass with its predictable permanency. Only the station of his chair ever moved, forward and back, never to one side, in rhythm with the washing advance and retreat of endless tides.

For several years, Emily and Clarence had passed him silently, without an extension of greeting. Often, Emily had wanted to speak but sensing a desire of privacy within him, she, with bitten lower lip, had withheld any salutation. Recently, however, gingerly, she had offered a cautious nod in his direction. It had been received politely with a similar bow of the head alone, accompanied by a slight smile, extended reservedly without further invitation for additional contact. She was delighted with the acknowledgement. Clarence was not surprised.

Heartened by his unpursued, return nod of greeting, Emily curiously sought to discover more about this stranger of the beach. One day, sniffing for clues, with a pumping squeeze of Clarence's hand, she directed their stroll, with sufficient leadtime disguise, on a detour behind the seated stranger in order to document the license plate on the rump of his faithful yellow compact car which always stood quietly by its master like a content camel ruminating on the sand, its four rubber hooves damply slotted with inlaid mosaics. The origin of the license plate was two counties away from the beach. Emily, a self-proclaimed Agatha Christie now, was quite smug with her findings. Gloatingly, she informed Clarence that indeed the stranger was not local but rather from the metropolitan county to their southwest.

"He comes at least forty miles, and perhaps sixty. We know that county," Emily asserted triumphantly, gesturing close to one eye with an invisible magnifying glass.

Clarence concurred. Clarence was not surprised.

Her case for the domicile of the stranger was strengthened soon thereafter when, on another late morning, as they passed, Emily had cunningly catalogued the banner of a small town newspaper, which was folded neatly across the arm of his chair, as indigenous to the county of the license plate. Without altering her methodical step, she had nosed in slightly, unobtrusively, below her straw sunbonnet to read above her bifocals, the bold, black banner.

The chair of the stranger had been vacated momentarily when Emily tallied the newspaper clue for her Exhibit B, as he had made another pilgrimage down to the booming surf, immersing himself to his leathery neck, after dashing his flatulent tummy with cuppy scoopfuls of cold water to inure himself to the shock of his icy bath. No other brave soul spotted anywhere on either horizon had ventured into the March water.

"That settles it, dear. He is from there," squealed Emily. "He drives that far every time. Isn't that amazing?"

"I'll grant you are right. It appears he comes that far," allowed Clarence. "Your laboratory evidence supports that fact." Pausing, he added with a chuckle, "Remember me, talking like my old prof' days?" He tenderly engulfed her chinadoll hand with his reminiscence.

Clarence had taught chemistry for twenty-eight years at a sedate, brick college, as proud and as straight as the mid-western corn which rose around it, all of those twenty-eight years. He never achieved the chair of his department as he had adroitly side-stepped political intrigue in the name of scholastic dedication. He had been revered by students and, much to the masked vexation of the starchy college hierarchy, his retirement a few years earlier had produced the largest alumni observance for a departing professor in the century-old history of the school.

In his caring life of service, Clarence had learned a great deal. One of the greatest things he had learned was if your bunions hurt, let them breathe through slit openings in canvas shoes. He was mindfully indifferent to the haughty stares evoked by his attempt at home cobblery. That was one of the reasons he never earned the department chair in chemistry.

Armed with her personal dossier of collected data, the solitary license plate and the damp, sandy newspaper, Emily, blithe and adventuresome, rallied a broad, twinkling smile when they drew abreast of the stranger the following weekend. Again he was pleasant with a boundaried, return greeting.

Upon closer inspection, the rusty chair proved not to be in disrepair at all, simply corroded and scaly from the bombardment of salt air. It was still quite utilitarian, like Clarence's canvas shoes. The stranger was dressed in baggy rayon shorts, supported by a groaning drawstring which warred against a tumbling belly, which had migrated southward in recent years for repose in perpetual winter, below the former vestige of a mighty chest. A clean, frayed, short terrycloth coat surrounded his upper body and a piece of toweling around his neck, tucked under the collar of the coat, protected him from the overhead, arching march of the relentless globe of glare.

The stranger had bundled up in recent years, necessitously now for survival, after a fusillade of snapping complaints with all doctors, and now daily shielded himself from the blind-white, scorching sun. With noticeable loss of pigmentation, his legs, with athletic evidence remaining, were motted with spots of brown and pale white swimming patchily upon them. Blood pressure medicine, prescribed for years, washing along with tincture of beer, had combined alarmingly in a catalytic reaction with the sun. The result had been a flaring bout with phototoxic poisoning. The stranger covered himself now, begrudgingly, fumy with the firm, medical decrees. However, his own prescription for beer remained unaltered. Other ingredients in the deadly formula were removed, but beer was never seriously considered as a prime candidate for removal.

The stranger sported a full Santa beard, gray-white, chopped sharply away from annoyance under his chin. It resembled a stage beard, as if detachable by two hidden ear loops of curved wire, as it hung there so incongruously with his total countenance. His square, burry haircut, flattop style of a generation once removed from the American scene, and a daily shaved upper lip, suggested perhaps a crack military bearing at one time in his life or at least, a mainstream business career, earlier at mid-century, before the new vogue of longer hair had become fashionable. His face, blotched in red and brown, was sharply featured, and emerging through the hirsute jungle of whiskers was archaeological evidence of a dashingly handsome younger man. He materialized, anachronistically, as our obscure, departed President Rutherford B. Hayes, bushily mutton-chopped, returning in the present century to attend a Pat Boone concert.

Beside the stranger in a similar folding chair, but tidily neater than his, one with crisp webbing and too new for much advancement in scaly corrosion, sat a short, stout woman, buttoned to her full chin in an assortment of sweaters and scarves, which were layered to her by a massive, tan coat. Her round, chubby face was soft with feeling, wisdom, and understanding. Although in her seventieth year, her oily skin, lubricating the creasing tendency of time, had slowed the aging lines of her face.

Wisps of white curls, fluttering in the ocean breeze, peeked out beneath a purple, woolen cap, which had been tugged securely well down upon her head. A thick library book, parted with half consumption, lay open upon her lap. Aslant against her shoulder, a plain umbrella with two bent spokes and a small, canopied window tear, partially repelled the sun, permitting her to read without the flashbulb-popping sun glare totally dancing away with the words. She was always with the stranger, beside him obligingly, but somehow over the years, Emily and Clarence had always referred to them as he, so striking to behold and to recount was his individual uniqueness of appearance.

Emily and Clarence were now fifty feet past them before she dared a whisper. A full head shorter than her husband, tiny, with matching elfin voice, she had learned over the years to wait until well outside the aural range of all possible unfriendly sensors before launching any of her innocent, pixie gossip for the flight up to Clarence's inclined receiver. The lesson had been forged years before, painfully, at the cruel anvil of college faculty parties. But, insouciant as Emily's harmless tongue might have been, Clarence's calloused bunions needed to breathe, and merciful breath they were permitted, well before Emily blundered and provided assistance for the blessed denial of any stuffy department chair.

"I wonder about them. To come so far each time. Wonder why? At least an hour's drive."

Emily had been an excellent mother, a culinary marvel, and a civic club stalwart throughout their active life in their former college town. Adding mightily to her charm, she often missed the most obvious reasoning with dainty, schoolgirlish oblivion, that pure, disarming variety that wears like Saturday clothes, comfortably, without inveigling design or conjuring motive.

Although she was his intellectual equal, Clarence had always been relieved that he had not been required to grade her for deductive reasoning as a student in any of his chemistry classes. He had loved her for her fine self and he had not complained about always reassembling her sketchy, scribbled notebook of the mind on the subject of empirical thinking. Charitably, without pontifical employ of red diacritical pencil, Clarence had cherished her without any attempt at fawning reconstruction.

"The beach is always changing. No two waves break in alike," began Clarence.

"To drive over every weekend day, my word," pursed Emily, unobservant to the lecture hour bell, silently ringing now for their outdoor, amphitheatrical classroom session.

"My classroom was always the same, near that clanking boiler room in the belly of the science building," began Clarence. "That morbid brown with the cracked blackboard. Somewhat like the water, always there, but the new students each year for twenty-eight years were the waves breaking differently, new people strolling by, a kind of interesting freshness each year that made me forget that cracked blackboard."

"You could have had a better room, dear," mothered Emily, with cute topical derailment, "but you wouldn't have been their person. You were a chemist not a politician. Besides, I never cared for those smart little receptions. Ghastly punch!

64

Never enough ice cubes. Your students coming by for my apple turnovers...now...ah!...those were my receptions. As for the cracked blackboard, humph, why lands alive, when you'd forget your lunch, I'd bring it along for you...why I never noticed that old blackboard once I knew it was there."

"What do you think about them?" jabbed Emily, tugging upon Clarence's billowy sleeve, proud of her blackboard soliloquy, while testing out poorly on the individuality of waves.

"Hm'm...," pondered Clarence, tapping a loose fist to his puckered lips, "I know I would like him. Them, that is. Him and her."

"You would? Why?"

"Yes, I would. They don't stare at my shoes."

"For that reason you can tell you would like them?" marveled Emily.

"Yes, most certainly. He, for instance, he knows what's important. He has made his peace with things."

"He has?" queried Emily, now wide-eyed and bent with total interrogative flurry.

"Yes. His things are old, clothes, belongings, but neat and orderly. I would say a retired businessman on a fixed budget in retirement. Independent, proud. Probably better off than his consumptive frugality would suggest, but afraid he might live too long and be a burden somewhere."

"How do you know these things? Are you using chemistry?"

"A lab of sorts," Clarence allowed. "A simple litmus paper test," chuckled Clarence, "from a fat notebook of data they provided themselves."

"You've lost me," muttered Emily. Her narrow, skimpy shoulders sighed reluctantly. Clarence squeezed her hand with surrounding encouragement.

"The book the woman was reading is a scholarly novel. The newspaper the other day, the one with the small town banner, was partly folded open at the financial page."

"So," concluded Clarence.

"So?" reiterated Emily, urging a spoon-fed meal of juicy morsels from Clarence's own detective story.

"People with intelligence, living plainly. An equation with a precipitate I like," mumbled Clarence.

"What was that, dear?" begged Emily.

"Oh! Nothing," dismissed Clarence with a trivial wave of his free, ocean side hand.

"But, why do they come so far, each time? Over an hour each way. Hardly easy. Wouldn't it be boring?"

"Vacations aren't boring."

"Vacations?"

"Yes, modest spenders. Good imaginations. Perpetual vacations. The gasoline to the beach is probably their only luxury."

"Imaginations now, goodness gracious dear," scolded Emily.

"His beach here is his Marrakesh, his Baghdad. His...his... uh, Paris, Rome, or London. A setting comforting and free, a vivid backdrop for his mind flight vacations in retirement."

"But, they must get tired of coming," persisted Emily.

"He, never. One can readily see. She, perhaps. Her books are her mind flight. She probably comes because of him."

"Tell, tell," squealed Emily.

"He's not afraid of dying. He's more afraid of not living if he didn't come. The sun has burned him and blotched his skin permanently. I'm not a physician, but I recognize, chemically, what happened to him. Still, he comes because his fanciful life is here. Some discomfort he has accepted. He's too hearty not to come. He has no vendetta with the sun which scarred him. He understands."

Clarence and Emily creaked past the lifeguard stand, a hundred yards up the beach from the stranger's little preserve of sand. They smiled up at the bronze Adonis lordly perched atop his wheeled sentinel stand of red. He acknowledged them politely with an enameled grin surfacing through a striped mask of white zinc oxide which rode wavily across his face over the bridge of his nose. He pitched his raucous radio blast decibels lower in deference to their senior passage.

"Well, I certainly would get tired of coming to the same place year after year," puffed Emily, unwilling to lay aside her drowsy theme.

Clarence smiled his whimsical smile, that silent companion of counsel fashioned from years as a professor, employed fatherly when the parade of hollow excuses for lost homework had trotted themselves by his pulpit of a desk in that dusky, sparse classroom.

They walked on silently, Emily spent with questioning, and Clarence resting from his rhetoric. Emily's tan feet were invigorated by the spill of chilling ebbtide and then numbed by needles when chancing clouds briefly abscounded with the sun. She wiggled her toes joyfully. Clarence's shoes were wet well up the canvas, his stockingless feet were unmistakably, but happily soaked.

Minutes later, fortified by silence, Clarence mustered his lecture summation as they approached again their quite mature, late middle-aged bug of an auto, parked there in patient wait upon the sand, ready to take them on the sputtering, coughing, four-mile drive across the causeway to their neat, stuccoed cottage on the quiet, shady street on the mainland.

"I've been thinking, Emily."

"Yes, dear."

"What say we stop our daily walks for a time? We've been on them now, just alike, for years."

"Oh dear! Perish the thought. Dismiss even the idea! We can't give up our walks, even for one solitary, single, itsy-bitsy day. Promise you won't mention it again. You have always said you loved them as much as my corn fritters."

She tugged at his sleeve again, more earnestly than before. Her enthusiasm jostled her sunbonnet, rainbowing briefly her thick eyeglasses, before patching a pleading eye with its newly tilted position. It did not dislodge against the wind. Clarence pressed it down tenderly upon her head.

"Why, our...our walks are...why, they are part of us. A vacation each day. Why, I couldn't give up my walks. My lands, they never get old!"

THE SUN
CAN
SHINE
AGAIN

In poky, wilting August, the black and booming sky of exhausting summer spat its late afternoon respite from infernal heat into flooding puddles upon the hissing asphalt parking lot. Crawling cars, with yellow eyes and slapping wiper lashes, unbedded these basins of rising water with their slowing tires disturbing perfect prisms of oily rainbows, sending miniature tidal waves on slurping, mischievious excursions about the feet and ankles of scampering shoppers.

Jim cautiously threaded his way down between two slanted rows of parked cars, craning his head through and around his droning wipers, which were losing the battle against successful rain repellency as the unforgiving sea often insults a puny dike of land. He could barely see the blurry forms of bracing, hunching shoppers, splashing to and from the equally blurry supermarket, which was a ghostly phantom of yellow and white haze, somewhere within the dark thunderstorm.

Marvelously near, traversing down only his second row, Jim plugged a vacating spot, which had happily opened with a surprise signal of red, exiting brake lights. Jim cut the engine he could scarcely hear, and slumped in his seat to ponder the rain. His fingers drummed a discordant tune upon his steering wheel. He sparked the ignition again and fumbled with the radio dial, and then, quickly, amid sharp atmospheric static, he yielded to the cracking staccato of ruined classical music, and shut off the knob in deference to the musical play of dreary rain upon the metal of his car.

Jim was smiling that anxious smile of confident anticipation, that blessed glow which totally overrides outside distractions, however uncomforting or disconcerting they may be. On the seat beside him, he casually thumbed through a stack of business papers which he had lugged home this Friday evening for routine inspection over the weekend; that is, inspection in its sequential preference, well behind television sports viewing, lawn puttering, and quiet naptime.

Then, with the rain still pelting down, he balanced his checkbook. This Jim did hurriedly, as that was the one odious little chore that was capable of sending his best, broad smile of confident anticipation off for an austere stay of interminable duration on the frigid Gulag. So, Jim dispatched with mercurial wonder the task of tallying escaping addition and hid his checkbook, save one check torn out for slippage into his shirt pocket, deep within his glove compartment, championing the weary axiom of "out of sight, out of mind". He slammed the tiny door and shook his jowls with his eyes tightly closed, as a father might react to his impolite offspring, eating with messy hands as a guest at Grandmother's home for Christmas dinner.

A renewed finger tapping of a haunting tune upon his steering wheel further repelled any insidious intrusion of forlorn concern with his flimsy checkbook. Jim rubbed a small porthole on his foggy window and peered through the gloom with a nose-pressing assessment for a wet, tactical dash to dry safety up to the protection of sidewalk in front of the stores. The sky was lightening a trifle, as it can miraculously do in the Florida summers, unlike the monotonous, all day nuisance rains of calendar winter there, which trail off begrudgingly with dripping perpetuity. He would make a run for it.

Jim glanced down at his well-traveled wingtip, cordovan dress shoes, soled and resoled at the bottoms, and just beginning to crack across the eyelets after fifteen years of periodic, though steadfast fondness for wearing. They would squeak for days once they got soaked, Jim allowed. He laughed aloud, still folded in his seat behind the wheel, at a comment made recently by his wife, a corporate whiz in industry, concerning his squeaky shoes.

At her plant, she had chided, management executives departing in afternoon rain, would prefer dashing to their long, shiny cars in stocking feet with their leather shoes tucked safely under an arm, than run the risk of having them shrink, for squeaking later down plush corporate carpets where every cautious step is tabulated for the possible privilege of future stardom.

Jim guessed it really boiled down to what was really

important to a person. Although he tried to look neat at his work, he damned for certain wasn't corporate. If his shoes squeaked for a few days after getting wet, he figured he could live with it. At least it would provide a joking topic of conversation if any business neighbor near his bland office suite chanced to poke a head in his doorway to visit.

With his air conditioning idle now for several minutes, the interior of the car was becoming stuffy, warming imperceptibly even with the dumping rinse of rain lowering the surface heat of the metal hood over the fizzing, settling engine. Jim glistened with perspiration, beading first across his forehead and upper lip, and then dampness, osmotically, stole about his neck, completely ringing his white collar. His dress shirt had a slight, gamy aroma, the result of several in and out excursions with his car, performed earlier on his appointment rounds during the blistering scorch of midday.

Jim unclouded another circle on his side window with his balled fist. The rain was slackening, falling straight down in its last hurrah, having surrendered to its previous, windy slant of fury. Jim made his snap decision, apologizing audibly once more to his shoes. Unfolding himself from his stiff, pretzed confinement, he bolted out his door. The stabbing rain was still fierce enough to pierce his back and shoulders like jagged needles of sharded glass.

His keys slipped through has hands and plunked into a puddle. Retrieving them, wet to his wrist, prompted a flood of epithets to no inclined human ear other than his own. He fumbled with the door lock as rain cataracted both eyes. Then, without running, he dog-trotted resignedly up to the raised sidewalk. The damage had been done with his dropped keys. There was no point in running, he was quite soaked. What was all that nonsense about running between raindrops, he groused privately with a frolicking grin, rebounding again to his happy mood with the episode of dropped keys quickly dispatched from his mind.

Standing on the protection of slippery sidewalk, streaky with foot passage, he shook his extended hands as fowl shake wings and blew a "whew" of relief from pouched, inflated cheeks. He ruled his wet hair with a brisk paw of massage as wet hair always revealed more visibly his receding hairline, and this fact invariably embarrassed Jim, so he jerry-built a tousled, dry head of hair, which passed for fullness, and felt better for it.

He fetched the limp, curling check from his shirt pocket, and clutching it gingerly with thumb and forefinger, fanned it dry in the air. Then, Jim made his way to the supermarket, down the treacherous sidewalk, a lurking snare for broken hips. He strode first past the familiar corner liquor store and furtively stole a glance in through the glass as a chaingang convict would look longingly at a passing, flippy skirt. He had tried not to look through these windows, but somehow his swollen tongue had swiveled his head all by itself. Jim grimaced and stumbled but somehow his wooden legs numbly carried him past to relative sanctuary once again.

He hastened past the dear, sweet old lady card shop and past the drug store, which seemed to offer everything from airline accident insurance to portable septic tank drain fields, in addition to maintaining a meager, jungle-hidden pharmaceutical counter somewhere at the rear of the establishment. He glanced in each store window successively, and with each passing store, the clammy shivering he had hated with his darting leer through the liquor store window, eased and then abated, until mercifully, he finally came to tremble no longer.

Jim swallowed hard and proudly entered through the whisking electronic doors of the supermarket as a triumphant king returns home to parting rows of bowing vassals after a successful crusade in a distant land. An Ipana-pleasant youth, with a military school haircut, and a sandpaper-scoured face of clean shave over a pustular battlefield of controlled acne, clankingly dislodged a shopping cart from a long, telescoped line of identical helpers, and genty shoved it in Jim's direction.

"You look happy today," the polite, young man offered as greeting.

"H'mm, guess I am, guess I am at that," ratified Jim. "Little wet, but won't melt, as they say. H'mm, guess I am happy," he repeated confidently. The cart attendant smiled after him, much of his way to the check cashing counter.

Jim knew all the uniformed gals at the check-cashing counter, which doubled as deposit bottle station, and tripled as cigarette carton Mecca. He often used the supermarket as a branch bank on his way home in the afternoon because he lived a goodly way from his real bank, but more necessitously, he used the supermarket as a bank because he was afraid to operate those satellite, robotic check-cashing devices. Jim had some talents in a few areas of endeavor, but success in being handy with any mechanical pursuit was certainly not one of them.

Fresh from high school, a quarter of a century earlier, as a raw, green recruit in Army basic training, he had posted the lowest score in his company of 210 men in the subject of manual dexterity and its application for Army skills, while posting, strangely, on the same testing day, the highest score among them all, in natural intelligence.

The commanding officer, after the testing, when Jim was informed he was eligible for officer candidate school, had scratched his head at his sparse, olive drab desk with Jim erect at attention before him, in saying, "I hope nobody ever assigns you to the motorpool if you ever become a lieutenant." When put at ease, Jim also had scratched his head, which sported a new, uneven swipe at a burr haircut, had tried to look flattered, but had remained a recruit.

Hastily his check was scrawled and plopped upon the ledge of the photographic device. He posed for his rogues' gallery enshrinement with his head tilted forward to firm up his slightly sagging chin. He liked to look presentable but the express purpose for his force of pose was to stage a little joke about his middle-aged chin, so he and the green-smocked clerks could have a little laugh. The Cyclopean lens eye snapped him with a riveting report that was as loud as a commercial stapler stamping a crate. He folded and pocketed his money and wheeled his cart down the far right aisle with

75

renewed singing in his heart.

He wove his way between a maze of parked carts, stationary in patient wait along the aisle, while their operators, ciphering housewives, methodically checked off budget items from their personal lists. He maneuvered as an adroit racecar driver, passing others on a crowded oval, with a faster machine under control.

What a bounty of liquid refreshment dazzled his eye. High to his left, shelved along the aisle, were neat rows of citrus fruit beverages, tinny cans and more graceful, curved-neck bottles of grapefruit and orange juice, those products indigenous to the Florida market. It had occurred to Jim several weeks before when he had started his new, twice-a-week ritual down this aisle, the first day of the rest of his life as he had begun to refer to it, that the citrus products had been placed there, strategically first to the eye, as designed inducement for local shoppers to be patriotic to their own state and also for new, relocating arrivals from other states, so they too could embrace their new home with patronage for state-grown products.

Of course! It was so obvious, but Jim had never stopped to ponder the fact, so busy had he been before this new pattern of shopping evolved, in selecting by rote, from another shelf in the market, the carbonated mixer that had been for years his toxic enemy's foaming partner in crime. Jim supposed that the positioning was somewhat like desserts at the beginning of a cafeteria line, arousing and titillating the palate when one was most hungry, sliding along an empty tray primed for some first selecton toward a meal.

Jim recalled the famous advertising book of his college days, Vance Packard's Hidden Persuaders, a theoretical monument about how advertising perks mold our subconscious minds. Quite pleased with his deduction, Jim halted his cart and mused for a brief instant, with a distant, pensive blankness drawn like a shade down over his happy face. Would he come to view other things differently, with perhaps a chance at greater clarity, once he had successfully traveled further down his new road. The thought intrigued him.

Jim passed up the citrus products. He had nothing against his home state, except those six month summers, and he was as patriotic as the next guy he supposed; however, his stomach ultimately made the choice against any citrus product selection. His stomach was just beginning to ungrumble like a reformed, enlightened Scrooge and Jim wanted to coax it along further, thankful to be waving adios to the peptic thunderstorm which had rumbled there periodically for years.

Just beyond the Siren-song of citrus products, Jim stopped his cart again. "Ah," he verbalized with museum-like piety. Seemingly enhaloed in angelic white light, the products from out-of-state, the eastern Appalachians, three states to the north, beckoned to him. They were three, valiant and righteous musketeers; apple juice, cranberry juice, and grape juice, there to protect and defend recovering stomachs of any realm.

His cart received its first hitch-hikers when a gallon of apple juice and another of cranberry were deposited carefully into the kiddie seat section. What a parade of enticing color those labels marched out for the purchasing dollar. Pulse-stirring, alluring pictures of luscious fruit sunning on mountain slopes, hypnotized the shopper with one subliminal, clarion call... HEALTH, HEALTH, HEALTH!

Jim slung a gallon of lowfat milk up into the cart from the other side of the aisle. The three, new acquaintances; apple, cranberry, and milk, bumped side-by-side down the gleaming tile floor to the end of the aisle. There Jim swung left, waved to the ladies behind the delicatessan counter, and saluted the two pot-bellied, tooth-picking butchers, who were lounging near the coldcut slicer in blood-stained, starched coats, watching the busy ladies do all the work.

Jim selected a free tidbit of diced Genoa salami and another of Swiss cheese from the display of snack trays arranged atop the counter. These snacks smiled down to passing shoppers with the innocence of an ingenue, but their presence translated instead to intended brisk, succumbing deli purchases all along the counter.

He looked for Granny, the senior citizen hostess employed by the supermarket as a Circean purveyor of all manner of delectable specialty items, designed to unfold your wallet and guaranteed to make your belt whine for a sharp-pointed awl. She was there beside her familiar freezer case along the spacious rear aisle, camped out defiantly like a sodbuster on a dusty prairie. Jim had come to chat with Granny on his rounds and almost always bought a package of something from her. She would launch into one of her stale persuasions, earnestly delivered across her creased, sun-browned face, and Jim would usually scoop up some little nicety from the cold, misting bin and add it to his moving pantry before she ever finished her selling plea. She thanked him each time as he departed with something, and Jim often would observe her tallying his little purchase with a pencil line neatly drawn on a napkin abacus she supposedly kept hidden from public viewing.

Jim hummed to himself along the meat counter at the rear, paraded past the free coffee urn without stopping to worship at the caffein shrine, and drew up to a full stop at the cola display on the end of a far aisle. There was a cola pricing war in progress, with more confusing tags and labels gestering about than signs jabbed in the air at political party conventions.

Jim noted all the specials, trying to decipher the myriad of bright arrows and hieroglyphic pointers with as much perplexing intensity as a trembling archaeologist hunched over a newly discovered, crumpling map, depicting possible ancient burial grounds. He hefted an 8-pak of clinking, 16-ounce bottles down from a high shelf and put them well down into the belly of the cart, wishing not to capsize his wheeled conveyance with further weight near his three gallons, which were gliding along safely in the kiddie seat section. The cola pricing was so enticing, Jim felt he couldn't refuse. Somehow, he always forgot the deposit on the bottles now that he was biting on those fantastic promotions.

Abruptly, the chameleon of change possessed Jim's happy

face. His cheek muscles tensed, cording his face with stratified definition. He shivered in the cool supermarket air. His fingers tightened with slipping dampness across the pushbar of his cart and he could sense again a slight pull of clinging wetness at the small of his back where his shirt, barely dry once more after the flight from the outside rain, began to blot against his skin with the ooze of new perspiration.

The gauntlet would have to be run, unless he cowardly detoured, in order for him to reach the checkout counters. Boldly, he chose to plunge ahead rather than to run away. Painfully, so painfully, it was getting easier, that gauntlet dash, that run through the hot coals of the mind, that naked passage for respectability, bludgeoned about the skull and shoulders by invisible sticks and cudgels. Like Dorothy seeking Oz with the trees alive with mocking, tentacled ensnarement along her route, Jim dared down the dark tunnel between the bottles of viperine refreshment with a hollow bravery, as one would shortcut to home late at night, whistling for companionship through an abandoned alleyway.

The longneck bottles of purple, red, and white were as silent as sentinels on night watch at a frontier fort. These last few weeks, their Poe-like eyes, seeing him pass, had gloated at the lingering ambivalence upon his face. Only lately had they become less smug, these seemingly gracile but treacherous sentinels, as the lingering doubt on Jim's face was losing territorial rights with each passage, and a confident new look, a knell of death for the longneck sentinels, was marching purposely across his face, in proud step to an accompanying faint drum roll of victory.

Jim scurried by the long, cold coffin, which was slunk off to his right in macabre repose of only feigned death. Its gelid breath rose eerily in a frosty mist. Foamy toxins in sarcophagi of aluminum, lay there in smirking ridicule, six to a bastard family, their stillness falsifying the devil arousement that lurked within them.

Suddenly, Jim was through and out the other end, mercifully free again and near the clacking registers, bathed anew seraphically in the white light at the front of the supermarket. He mopped his beading forehead with the back of one hand. His jelly legs thanked another part of his body for a transfusible donation of blood. The hissing cans and gurgling bottles clattered in livid rage with his escape and moaned with their new shortened, unreaching grope for imprisonment.

With two brown sacks, one in each arm, Jim passed through the electronic doors again. The two juice gallons had taken up lodging with the milk and Granny's frozen deli concoction rode piggyback in the other bag, on the shoulders of the eight bottles. The rain had abated greatly, with only drooling drizzle remaining. The sky was yellowing with rips of sunlight slashing through the spent shield of gray.

Clusters of shoppers milled outside, chattering together on the wisdom or folly of breaking for their cars with the rivuleting lakes eager to drench indiscriminantly even the most judiciously placed shoe. Many, with frozen goods beginning to melt, decided on discomfort and peeled off one by one for a wade to their cars with plaintive, resigned goodbyes to those who remained behind, timidly rooted to the relative dryness of the sidewalk.

Jim paused only briefly, knowing full well that he would wade to his car. He reflected only to sing in his heart again, for another glorious moment. He basked in his outside surroundings, ignoring the oily ocean lapping up against the sidewalk, as he was savoring the victory won again this day inside the store, that renewing, twice-a-week victory down that dark, narrow tunnel of aisle. The skies for Jim were parting with the spellbinding, crinkle-magic of the old, metal curtain in his boyhood theater.

With the mimicking dance of Gene Kelly, without the umbrella, expert dance steps, or resonant voice, he tapped off the sidewalk curbing down into the waiting footbath immersion, singing undauntedly in his heart. Some people gasped, others were indignant with his childlike buffoonery, but a precious few, perhaps those remotely familiar with his kind of unbridled flight for the mind, applauded his antics with shouting kudos, substituted necessitously for parcel-busy hands, which were indisposed for clapping.

Jim retraced his arrival path, followed in the opposite direction twenty minutes earlier, however, this time, he was wading freely in the parking lot in front of the sidewalk. He inclined his face upward in the returning blue and orange sky,and rotated his neck and face in the warmth. The dull ache at the base of his neck was gone. He relished the Friday evening awaiting him. He wouldn't have to take three tablet slugs of acetylsalicylic acid before tumbling into bed to aid his wheezing organs in their attempt to siphon morning pain from his brain. He wouldn't have to see his eyes in the mirror on Saturday morning, barely discernible beneath shoveled piles of deep compost.

He gamboled by the drug store, then the card shop, pirouetting oafishly with his two brown sacks unbalancing his little dance, and drew abreast of the liquor store on the corner, still sloshing in the asphalt lake.

The two attendants inside the liquor store were standing near the front, by the glass doors. They had no customers at the moment. The rain had dampened sales for an hour and the arrival of the rollicking stream of construction workers for their bagged cache of Friday afternoon beer for their spirited trek home was still another half-hour away. The two men were enjoying the V-shaped wake of sputtering cars and the carnival parade of disgruntled shoppers tiptoeing miserably to their unsympathetic cars.

With his carouseling antics, Jim's arrival within the scope of their view was quite obvious to them. The senior citizen clerk, angular and gaunt, with purple, dappled hands taloned at the end of scraggy, bony arms queried his associate, a much younger man, the son of the store owner.

"Where's he been? Several weeks now, ain't it? Been out some myself with them damn stones but he ain't shown, has he?"

"Dunno," snapped his shorter companion, laconically. He always grunted around his fellow workers, saving his dulcet tones for paying customers. "Been one of our best. Two jugs a week for years," he lamented with hands akimbo upon his hips with resolute family business curiosity.

"That's right, sure 'nough," sighed the old man comtemplatively, tapping out a filterless cigarette from a crumpling pack.

"Look at him, crazy as ever," smarted the son. "Where the hell is he buying his hooch," he pondered with vested family indignation.

The senior citizen, a tired warrior of military, beergarden duty and then a dreary decade of lousy saloon jokes before achieving the relative sanctuary of surburban liquor store sales, answered dryly, with an undesigned hint of whimsy.

"Maybe he ain't. Seen it before. Rare though, with them heavy ones."

The old man drew a thin, tentative hand subconsciously across his abdomen, winced, ballooned foul air in his mouth over white gums, and shuddered with a cough.

ONLY AN OCEAN APART

Sitting alone, reading, in the darkly paneled smoking lounge of his private club, Jerome Abernathy was bored. He could hear the muddled chorus of late afternoon laughter drifting to him from around the corner in the adjoining bar and scarcely cared if their gossipy banter involved him. Nervously, he shifted his feet on the elegant sward of rich carpet beneath his deeply padded, wine-red chair. Jerome was exhausted, not from hard work but rather from the avoidance of it. With the index finger of his right hand, he squeakily explored, round and round, the circular rim of the tall cocktail glass beside him. With his left hand he snatched hungrily through the sleek, crackling pages of the fashionable travel magazine perched on his lap.

Jerome had completed that afternoon three agonizing weeks of closed-door, hammer-tough sessions with punctilious city and county dignitaries, battering out for his father, the force behind the largest road paving company in southern California, the final details for the upcoming expressway improvement project. The contract had been awarded to the family firm and was to be the largest paving contract ever voted for southern California.

For fifteen weekdays, Jerome had endured those meetings. Often, his elbows, derricking his ample chin, had slipped from the edge of the room-sized, mahogany conference table, causing his neck to jerk forward violently. Miraculously, each time he had recovered without being embarrassed. Wearily, through the three-week drone of windy dictum, he had daydreamed exotic flights of fantasy elsewhere, on every continent, in swank restaurants where imaginary toothpicks were collected in each to prop open his leaden eyes. Seemingly, every ward person, every council member, obscure or flamboyant, dozingly hypnotic or self-aggrandizingly obnoxious, had added their own sermon to the proceedings as if they were protecting themselves against prying perusals made later by any nosy, record-studying constituency.

Happily, the long ordeal had ended that afternoon and now there would be a two month respite for engineering detailing, before the gigantic project would officially lurch forward with the legions of sweat-stained, denim-clad men and their phalanxes of oily, thundering earth-moving machines clattering noisily under the supposed watchful, caring eye of Jerome. The thought of standing out on the hot, clamorous job site made him nauseous. The project would last fully two years. He loathed the snarl and clash of heavy machinery.

Jerome sighed langourously, and moodily gazed at his glass of foaming toxin and then about him at his grand surroundings. His eyes slowly surveyed the lounge, beginning with a vainglorious, narcissistic inspection of his embroidered smoking jacket, daily brushed and periodically steamed by a steward, ready always in his wall locker for late afternoons when he came to collapse at the club.

Exquisite wall coverings adorned down from the high, vaulted ceiling until their tapestried richness met the elegant, waist-high, paneled wainscot. Antique, polished spittoons, never dirtied, and neatly arranged magazine racks graced each plump leather chair, like supportive bookends. The chairs were assembled in a feigned random, but resulting orderly, wide fashion before a stone fireplace, from which a perpetual blaze of imitation fire flickered, year round, amid the icy, air-conditioned maintenance of the room.

He rued his approaching duty, and struggled not to think about the perfunctory show of interest he would have to fake in two short months, inspecting boiling asphalt spreaders which tortured his olfactory nerves, and the rumbling, shuddering Goliathan machines which assaulted similarly his auricular senses.

Jerome was a rich man but his wealth did not set him free. Equestrian and fencing lessons for his two sons, ballet and voice instruction for his two daughters, none of whom were talented even a smidgen in any of the four pursuits, were administered like castor oil to a feverish child. An endless parade of summer camps, private tutors, and the pecking order accoutrements of showy teenage baubles, decreed an unpardoning sentence for Jerome on the dusty construction sites.

He put the pink palm of his drink-free hand to his forehead and steadied his swaying head as the shopping list of his wife's expensive play things was tabulated. Her decorator, her masseuse, her dressmaker, her bridge-playing excursions, her jaded haunts of clubs and cliques, all tallied unmistakably to an endless future for Jerome at those blind-white concrete stretches, at least until his father decided upon a different role for him or died. He hardly gave a damn that he was the sole heir to the largest road building operation in California.

Jerome's father, Carl, the son of late 19th century Celtic immigrants, had come west in the early 1930's, between the great wars, in search of an opulent future, after vagabond excursions with lumberjacking and merchant marine stevedoring in the Northeast. Ribbons of concrete, lattice work with muscle, were starting to lace together southern California, nudging and poking through trim orange groves and sleepy little towns. The movie industry was well established but the real estate boom, the real one after the "roaring 20's" fizzle, was yet to materialize. When it mushroomed after the Second World War, Carl was there, opportunely, straddling its weed-like proliferation with brawny shoulders hulking over a feet-apart resolute stance, primed and expectant for success at any price.

Carl had started at the end of a shovel in the 1930's and had survived in a flophouse, where his hoarded, meager dollars, hidden in his pillow, were invested as a part interest in a mobile sandwich business for construction workers. He laminated dry, gummy sandwiches by night and underpaid Mexican-Americans hawked them at noon to his fellow workers. Carl had remained a silent partner and never, on the job, were his glowing endorsements of the vendored sandwiches ever fathomed as deep-pocketing rhetoric by his unsuspecting customers.

During the Great Depression, he worked two jobs and bought a handshake share in a light equipment venture, through which he and others leased back machinery to his employer when, strategically, company machines began to flounder in drydock motor pools with mysterious missing parts. He befriended the right people and even engineered a whirlwind romance with the daughter of a physician at the beginning of the war for the express purpose of cadging a 4F diagnostic letter from her father on his perfectly fine hearing, that he claimed had become damaged, somehow, from the bleating foghorns of merchant marine vessels during his early years with the fleet.

Carl wasn't unpatriotic. He would challenge anybody, anywhere, who was infringing on his own grubstake or invading his own sacred turf. He understood the protection of claimed domain in the private, personal sense. He just couldn't see going off to war on hostile foreign soil with all those juicy defense and construction contracts forthcoming for southern California. Carl stayed home. During the war, he expanded his power base and finally broke free on his own with work guarantees wrestled from suppliers who glumly realized that Carl knew of their brown bag transfers of hush-money payoffs.

When the war ended, Carl worked feverishly for a few more years, into the 1950's, with stumble-weary dedication. By then, the influence of his company was unstoppable. The burgeoning growth, practically devoid of zoning restraint, was unchecked and Carl, while Jerome was still a boy, was able to discard his chalky work clothes for the trappings of a full-fledged, nouveau riche effete. He was uproarious with his meteoric economic ascent. Old friends were spurned and expensive dalliances unwrapped with consumptive ostentation.

Carl groomed Jerome for future stardom with the company. Jerome, however, displayed few traits of his father. He showed no knack for chicanery with city officials and no blustering bravado with competitors. He demonstrated absolutely no aptitude for duplicity with establishment "movers and shakers". Carl tried repeatedly, probing the spacy, inner workings of Jerome, trying to unleash on the unwary world the "artful dodger" he hoped lurked elusively within him. It was to no avail. In a few years, as Jerome grew to college age, Carl came to rationalize the whole disappointment wistfully, concluding that real talent sometimes skips a generation and this was what had happened with Jerome. Carl became almost pleased with his solid pivot to deductive wisdom on the subject of Jerome's shortcomings. It absolved him from any direct genetic blame.

With a very generous allowance, Carl shipped Jerome back across the country to a swank Eastern college and tried to forget about him. He immersed himself in the pleasure of his empire to savor the sweetmeats of his bounty and wearily pigeonholed the thought that in four years, after Jerome had finished college and was jerry-built, sketchily, for the business world, he would have to select the correct, innocuous cubbyhole in which Jerome could bustle, collide, and sputter, doing nothing to sink the company.

Carl started him in architecture; Jerome detoured to civil engineering and the college, aghast at his ubiquitous ineptitude, gracefully led him to mechanical drawing where cloaked plots with department heads predetermined Jerome as an eventual "gentleman C" graduate, in the fervent hope that father would be a future source of generous bequests for the college.

Jerome interacted with all the sons of famous "downeast" families but their tolerance for him was short-lived and he was politely avoided at every opportunity, as was to be his eventual ostracism later, at clubs and gatherings. Initially, Jerome wasn't disturbed. He didn't understand the polite, side-stepping powders he was handed by practically everyone.

All the important young men came up to his dormitory room to listen to records and to smoke foreign cigarettes. Carl had coached him on the subtle art of seeking and knowing the right people. Jerome, obligatorily, had cross-referenced the school student list with the bluebook social register Carl had provided, in order to select the correct guests for music and smoking.

Because Jerome was seldom invited back anywhere, he had plenty of leisure time to poke about the quaint shops in the old colonial city, with his bulging monthly allowance suffocating in his wallet begging to be spent. The endless stream of coaxed, seldom returning, victims enjoyed the foreign cigarettes and the music. In not realizing that their true acceptance of him was hopeless, Jerome set about stocking his room with cartons of exotic tobaccos. But his real pursuit for ornaments of attraction, glitter wampum for their reluctant, abbreviated shuffles up to his place, was phonograph records.

Jerome combed every record store and purchased a prodigious array of music. He became monomaniacal over records. His room became a warehouse of stacked boxes. His scoffed reputation spread to the limits of the campus. By the conclusion of his sophomore year, everybody, who was anybody, knew that Jerome had the largest phonograph collection on campus and perhaps in the entire city. When boxes cluttered his room making movement impossible, Jerome would ship the boxes in crates to his father. Initially, Carl balked at their arrival but when Jerome's letters arrived almost simultaneously, describing without conjured design all the important young men who were enjoying the music, Carl's acquisitive vanity for power bested reason and he accepted and stored the crates, and maintained Jerome's monthly stipend without compunction.

Vanessa was handpicked by Carl to be Jerome's wife. After graduation, as Jerome accustomed himself to his austere, lifetime sentence with the construction company, he was steered unveeringly toward Vanessa. Unlike Middle East folklore, this princess, essentially predetermined in childhood as Jerome's future wife, was no shy, retiring goddess of allure. Reedy, with streaky, blondish hair and skin that cracked like saddle leather wearing in the sun, Vanessa, the oldest daughter of a mother from the legitimate Broadway stage and a father who had pinched a fortune in the corset business, was Carl's perfect selection for Jerome.

Carl had watched her mature. He liked her flit at cocktail parties, her disarming sarcasm, her piercing hyenic laugh, her pedigree from the legitimate theater, and her uncanny ability to deliver a stream of seamy gossip at the bridge table while playing with tournament caliber aplomb.

They were married and Jerome was told he would be happy. Vanessa went to bed and stayed for months with each of her four pregnancies. After her childbearing years, she, with the provided luxury of a stern, "old world", Lithuanian governess and a huffy, boarded tutor, largely abandoned her four children to a future date with friendless snobbery and ravenously refined her world-class bridge talents.

Much to Jerome's chagrin, as he had dearly hoped for at least a legitimate friendship with her, Vanessa won a spot on the California traveling bridge team and her luggage, thereafter, turned up plastered with stickers from every major city on every continent in the world except Antarctica. Her ruffed jack in Rio de Janeiro beat the Brazilian team at the Western Hemispheric Championships; her 27-point final hand turned away the Italians at Milan; and every wagging tongue owned by every sun-weathered, anorexigenic hostess at liquor bashes all over southern California repeated her 127 cigarette ordeal, waiting out the South Africans at the twelve-hour final set-session win in Johannesburg.

From his soporific, cushy chair Jerome crankily rang the bar buzzer with his foot, telegraphing a drink request around the corner, as he snatchily continued to prowl through his magazine with the undercurrent of bar laughter mocking his consciousness. The only real laugh Jerome ever fashioned for himself at the club was the night he slurred, through vodka gimlets, his woes cf curious Vanessa peeking and peering into all his private matters. His cornered group at the bar had roared spontaneously when he had blurted, "She opens everything, my bank book, my safe in the study, my mail, my safety deposit box. The only thing of mine she doesn't open anymore is my fly."

Jerome was unaccustomed to originating a full-bodied, genuine laugh through cleverness so it pleased him greatly to entertain briefly that night. But Jerome wouldn't leave it alone. He dropped the solitary, cute one-liner as bait for new conversations on ensuing nights and soon he had sent scurrying off again any hope of even lukewarm alliances.

Charles, the regiment-erect and saber-thin blade of a waiter, wordlessly delivered Jerome's fifth vodka gimlet of the evening and placed it beside him with a brisk nod and a stiff salute with his tray. Jerome had pillaged through the travel magazine, crumpling pages, reading nothing, sampling longingly in his mind the sensual call of far away places of enchantment, enticing the eye through magical settings of high adventure.

Toward the rear of the magazine his eye caught an advertisement. He sat up, as straight as possible, and leaned aslant toward the low light near his drink in order to distinguish the fine print. It read:

PHOTOGRAPH THE BIG FIVE
AFRICAN GAME ANIMALS
--CAMERA SAFARIS--
CAPTURE ON FILM ELEPHANT, RHINO,
CAPE BUFFALO,
LION AND LEOPARD
CHARTERS - SUMMERS - KENYA

The derisive laughter around the corner at the bar, shrill and aggressive, bouyed by alcoholic caper, reddened Jerome's ears. No one was smearing Jerome verbally but he always imagined they were. He read on with mounting curiosity, peeved with his conspicuous insularity in the lounge.

COMFORT ACCOMODATIONS - EXPERT GUIDES
ADVENTURE AWAITS THE ADVENTURESOME

Jerome had a rare revelation. He shifted bolt upright again

and inadvertently touched off the foot buzzer, well before the required time for his sixth drink. He could go. Vanessa was in Glasgow for a month at the British Championships and his four children, save one in remedial summer school French, had been shipped shriekingly off to dude ranches all across the West. The road project wouldn't start until October. He winced again at the thought of that white helmet with the plastic liner that always hurt his temples and those starched, brown khaki pants, chafing his fleshy inner thighs.

Madly he devoured the remainder of the advertisement. His eyes darted across the page.

EXCURSIONS FOR FILMING
OTHER GAME ANIMALS
THE ANTELOPES -- THE GREAT APES
SEE THE DARK CONTINENT NOW!

He would go! It was settled. Jerome hurried from the smoking lounge, still wearing his brocaded jacket, and turned and exited through the bar without waving goodbye to anyone. No one there had any intention of first acknowledging Jerome. He fairly ran through the parking lot, causing arriving dinner members to stare inquisitively at his smoking jacket, with its loop-stitched lapel and cuff gaudiness quite out of place outside amongst the cars.

Jerome set his jaw hard and ground his teeth. If the largest phonograph collection in the lousy country wasn't enough, topped off with his priceless one-liner about Vanessa, he would give them something more. He would show them. How many of those booze hounds had photographed the dangerous game animals of the world? He would have a complete collection, just like his phonograph records and that would include, he determined with totality, the antelopes too that the magazine mentioned.

*   *   *

93

Ernest Rutherford, freckled, carrot-haired, and outdoor ruddy was a third generation Englishman in East Central Africa. His father and grandfather before him had been big game hunters and guides but with the focal consciousness about the world in Ernest's time for the protection of endangered species, Ernest, himself, had been compelled to pivot to camera safaris for survival. Armed now with a black shutter box and not a powerful elephant gun, he had felt emasculated, early on, as if he had violated a family tradition, but with the passage of time, fifteen years now photographing not killing, he had mellowed from guilt and, with a new appreciation for live animals, unthreatened by camera in their natural habitat, he had come to champion their protected existence without further apology to his deceased paternal lineage.

Ernest, stocky, of middling height, sporting a bushy, orange upper lip, wore traditional tan khaki shorts, olive-drab, woolen knee socks, and couldn't be separated from an old family heirloom - a jaded, frayed, white bush jacket, with a stitched half-belt at the waist and a parade of bullet loops across the front. The loops hung idly now, devoid of the steel-jacketed bullets for which the loops were sewn thirty years before and only one loop served any real purpose, as a substitute sleeve for Ernest's omnipresent Calabash pipe.

Jerome had wired money ahead, indeed more money than required. With that happy circumstance, Ernest, curious about his windfall surprise, personally met Jerome at the airport. Usually he sent his official greeter, Ujiji, the Ugandan guide who had faithfully served Ernest and his father for nearly half a century. Ernest scarcely knew how to utter a greeting when Jerome deplaned, so accustomed was he in having Ujiji and sometimes his entire porter retinue meet new charters with hastily donned tribal regalia, spears and shields in hand for show, and with facial markings smudged where Western after-shave lotion customarily lurked. Ujiji and the others always howled a protest to Ernest when he made them dress unnaturally for the gullible Americans. They much preferred their designer jeans and checkered Maine guide shirts but they performed reluctantly when goaded, always laughing uproariously afterward at the American naivete' for their totally staged drama. Ernest didn't make them endure the ritual very often anymore. Its falseness had come to bother him.

Two vehicles, one a nine-seat Landrover with an erectable camera portal projecting through the roof, and the other, a larger support, utility truck, reminiscent of an old Western chuck wagon, replete with tents, folding chairs, a purified water tank, a pantry of delicatessan delights, sterling silver place settings, linen tablecloths, and one cast-iron bathtub, nudged out ostentatiously from civilization, northwest bound, the following morning at dawn. The utility vehicle boasted the only portable, self-contained, ice-making machine in East Central Africa.

All of Ernest's rich American clients seemed to be two-fisted drinkers and nothing, save perhaps a hot bath in the bathtub at end of day, was quite like sunset on safari, slumped in a campchair with a drink in hand, after a jostle-jangle full day rodeo in the Landrover.

Jerome could have outfitted himself with khakis from the job site at home but instead he purchased a needless wardrobe of stylish bush clothes the day he arrived. Also carefully stored among Jerome's personal possessions for the trek were two cases each of quinine water and tonic, nine liters of vodka, a quart jar of Milk of Magnesia tablets, and a foot-high stack of faded, crumpled, and sufficiently dog-eared Penthouse magazines.

The vista stretching before the beetle creep of the two vehicles was majestic. Open, rutted clay trails ribboned without end over undulating expanses of lion-tan grass, which shimmered with purple and turquoise hues of dance. Kaobob trees, gaunt and stark against the sky, huge, with their limbs sprung like the splayed fingers of giants, stood well apart, like feuding prairie neighbors. Their lower trunks were marred roughly from the back scratch of elephants. Herds of grazing ungulates, the homely wildebeests and their equally unattractive cousins, the hartebeests, roamed in swarming, dust-stirred throngs, swinging one direction and then another in parade-band unison, with their alert and air-sampling heads carefully raised, ever searching for water and more importantly, for any possible surprise ambush from stalking lions.

Jerome stood as Ernest drove, his shoulders protruding through the roof opening, while he surveyed the vast expanse of gentle plain, like lordly Rommel reviewing his desert troops. Balancing himself against the bucking lurch of the Rover, Jerome trimphantly savored his display of power and importance. Two cameras jangled in collision about his neck. He gleefully shouted with exuberancce as a military plebe on his first holiday, and the memory of Vanessa, his object-grabby offspring, and the road project were erased from his consciousness for a time.

Away from civilization, the first day out, Ernest spotted Jerome's first camera trophy. The dangling, rigid legs of a young antelope caught his trained eye. A female leopard was feasting on this fresh kill twenty feet high in a barren, thirsty tree. Ernest wheeled the Landrover within fifty yards, knowing the hungry leopard would not skittishly abandon her prize. Jerome clicked madly, protected by the casing of vehicular metal. The leopard snarled defiance with bared fangs and flattened ears and her limp dinner swayed precariously on the bobbing limb.

The following day, in the late afternoon after 40 miles of investigatory driving through drying creek beds and rock-strewn gullies, the plod-heavy, lumbering gait of an African rhino was detected, shying away in an acre-sized clump of chest-high bushes. Ernest pursued the rhino in ever cinching maneuvers, as yelping Indians once circled drawn-together Conestoga wagons. The rhino, three tons of tank-tough fury, grew tired of Ernest's game and broke from cover to pace the Landrover directly alongside of it.

Jerome had a lens broken when the thrashing, anvil-sized head of the rhino butted the Rover repeatedly as the beast paralleled Ernest's circumnavigations. Jerome, only feet above the brute, squeezed off pictures with one hand, while using his chin as a second camera appendage, in place of the other arm that was clinging desperately to the pitching vehicle. The rhino tired quickly and suddenly shuddered to a halt, completely fatigued, and stood quivering with exhaustion. Pints of slimy saliva drooled from its panting, oblong snout, and only flaming eyes, ingot red, and twitching ears spoke its anger and frustration. Ernest inched the Rover again within thirty yards and cut the engine. The rhino moodily declined further jousting and, mustering now only feeble bravado, chose not to flee.

"Bang, bang," chortled Jerome, squealing as a schoolboy at playground recess. He fashioned a pistol with his hand and poked it toward the rhino. Ernest abhorred Jerome's puerile manner and backed away slowly from the spent pugalist, choosing not to add to its agony.

Ernest now hated guns and their destruction. He did not fault his father and grandfather for their taking of trophies in their era. But now this was his era and the same slaughter was not sanity, only utter lunacy. The spread of the dusty Sahara far to the north seemed to encroach southward a little more each year, imperceptibly adding more arid acreage to Africa. The assimilation of native cultures by Western influences had not benefited the land. Tourism with its tawdry congestion was rising relentlessly and the animals seemed to sense the intrusion. The great, milling herds, clouding the sky with stirred dust from their million-footed trample, were more elusive to locate and were methodically dwindling in numbers.

Ernest warred with himself on the topic of dwindling game. Was it the expectancy factor feverishly at work in his brain, creating seemingly fewer animals to behold, or was it actually happening? The dilemma was maddening to a caring Ernest, and the knowledgeable people he quizzed on the subject gave conflicting, divergent answers, adding to his unsettledness.

Early each evening with two hours of full daylight remaining, a campsite, near water, would be selected for the night. Ujiji and his crew would swoop into action like circus roustabouts at pink dawn. Wall tents were erected and roped fast, thorn bushes were cut and readied for their entrances to ward off any wayward, carnivorous feline chancing by to inspect slumbering occupants in the dead of night.

Ernest and Jerome bathed unhurriedly, one after the other, Jerome first, with two natives assigned to change the water and to scour the cast-iron tub between the two blessed submersions for the dust-caked Caucasians. With lanterns illuminating, the evening meal always was a full course banquet served on sterling silver, arranged over a flapping, white linen tablecloth spread across tables that folded out. But dinner was always late, served at full darkness, permitting a long, leisurely cocktail session for Ernest and Jerome. Their chairs, canvas Hollywood-director types, were faced before the unspooling, glorious sunsets, somewhat away from the campfires, as escaping smoke irritation was impossible to predict.

"And your record collection is the largest in California?" meditated Ernest.

"Without question," Jerome assured smugly. "And maybe the largest anywhere when the new shipment comes in."

"New shipment?"

"Yes, boxes and boxes. Four hundred albums."

"Of what?" pursued Ernest.

"They call it cross-over country and then there's green grass, uh, no, bluegrass they call it. Never heard of the stuff but it will make mine the biggest collection, I'm positive."

"The biggest," repeated Ernest, repacking his pipe with thumb and forefinger while his great leonine head of orange slanted searchingly, masking a pitying smile, emerging only to himself below the surface of his countenance. "When do you have time to listen to all your records?" explored Ernest, intrigued.

"Oh! Goodness," laughed Jerome, "I haven't played five percent of them. Never will. Too many. It's hard enough cataloging and filing them away in my vault. Temperature

98

controlled, you know."

"Temperature controlled?"

"Oh, yes. Not like a florist, nothing like that, but it never gets above 72 degrees in there."

Jerome yawned and trudged off to his tent. Ernest sat for a time, alone, and nursed the sputtering fire until only glowing embers, like the blazing eyes of the great cats, remained.

"Crossover country and bluegrass," Ernest murmured privately. "Coming in boxes, opened only for display." He spat contemptuously into the low fire. It hissed back meekly.

A bull elephant, as tall as a basketball goal, with laden ivory sweeping to the ground like cutting sickles, was photographed two days later at eighty yards distance. The gray behemoth, with ears flapping like canvas sail in a breeze, had trotted toward them, away from his knotted herd, for a closer inspection of their intrusion. With Jerome clicking wildly, Ernest kept the motor running and addressed his excellency at right angles in case an immediate, hasty retreat became imperative.

Later the same day, the fourth prize promised Jerome was flushed into view along a drying creek bed. Ernest had piloted the Landrover, in low gear for several miles, in and out of slapping grass and bramble, which barely remained alive along the puny drinking edge of the gasping trickle. The Cape buffalo, with furious, beady eyes, appearing small by contrast below the brow swagger of prominent horns, emerged, startling their little caravan. They were six in number, two bulls and four calves. Their snouts hung threateningly, swayed nervously and water dripped rudely from their slit mouths, which were caked wet with mud.

Now, among the five main prizes to be filmed, only the king himself, the lion, remained for Jerome's camera. Their success had come swiftly, days before Ernest's scheduling for it. Surely Jerome, with their present good fortune, would extend the camera safari, concluded Ernest, beyond what had been accomplished, to include filming the antelopes. It would be nice to win additional commissions now, instead of returning early to Nairobi for another greenhorn American.

Jerome boasted his success that evening in camp. He recounted hyperbolically each filming victory over an extended melee with vodka and tonic as Ernest and he sat again as Hollywood tycoons below a scatter of blue-ice, diamond stars amid a cast of thousands, milling invisibly across the immense, darkened veldt, freely acting at the casting whim of no human director.

"The lion will be the easiest," pronounced Ernest, "the vultures will point him out. A road map that seldom lies. We'll be done with over two weeks left."

"No!" squealed Jerome. "I want the others too, uh, the uh, those others. That-that one named after a car. The impala. You promised."

"Oh, the antelopes," corrected Ernest, wondering again why he endured such asinine rubes as Jerome. One day soon, hopefully, he would retire from his bush wanderings. He sighed mightily, as a man with a heavy load with no immediate place on which to set and rest it. "Yes, the antelopes," recited Jerome.

"We can do it," replied Ernest with theatrical nonchalance. "With the water holes drying up, they'll all film fine. Together, most. Kudu, the giant eland, impala, springbok, Grant and Thompson gazelle." Ernest felt foolish repeating their names. Jerome would remember only impala as named after a car.

"Let's do it then," shouted Jerome.

"We'll save the okapi for last," finished Ernest. "He's three hundred miles up in the forest, northwest of here."

"O-ka-pi," mouthed Jerome haltingly, tripping over the syllables.

"Yes, I told you, remember? The first day riding out. If you get the okapi, it means more than the rest of the antelopes together."

"Rare, elusive," instructed Ernest. "Distinctive markings. Creamy white leg stripes on reddish-brown hide. Giraffe family. About five feet high."

100

Ernest raised a course palm of one hand parallel to the ground as he sat.

"That's the prize you'll treasure. Wasn't even seen by Europeans until about 1900."

The male lion reposing within his hierarchical pride, was readily located below circling vultures just before noon the following morning. By ear, the maniacal, chilling laugh of the slope-shouldered hyena also oriented the location. The scavengers were beginning to pick clean a zebra kill.

The vultures flapped down from the air, practicing their touch-and-go landings, and strutted in to feed voraciously among the jackels and hyenas, which surrounded the disappearing zebra, like radiating spokes of a wheel.

With protruding belly, his majesty dozed sixty yards away. Clouds of buzzing flies swirled about his gamy muzzle, which still reeked from the residue of warm flesh consumption. In near slumber, when the flies annoyed his satiated state of indifference beyond tolerance, his great mane would fly about as the disheveled hair of an eccentric conductor, extracting a fortissimo from his orchestral charges.

Three lionesses, the real assassins for the lordly feast, reclined together, stretching and purring nearby, and they licked their paws meticulously as if to eradicate all evidence of their necessary, murderous deed. Their cubs, with youthful exuberance, gamboled like playground ruffians, tumbling over one another as curled balls, with puny snarls for show alone.

Jerome had settled upon the antelopes as a final tribute to his trip. The road construction project was nearly a month away and he ciphered the loss of only two days with return travel and accompanying jet lag. The glamour of the okapi prize intoxicated him. Like the new albums of crossover country and bluegrass awaiting him at home, those pictures would render him unique indeed, set him apart, and win for him the adulation and envy of his acquaintances. He would show them.

Ernest had warned that the okapi tracking would be

arduous with much of the camera pursuit on foot in the forest uplands where the open, burning veldt abdicated reluctantly to a welcome, cool canopy of foliage.

They drank together again that evening as they had every twilight. A glorious pink, orange sky retreated to a sliver of violet and then disappeared as full darkness within the sleeve of a magician. A dusty, full-day drive of three hundred, lurching miles awaited them at dawn.

"I appreciated classical music as a young man," offered Ernest, seeking to further explore again this additional evening, Jerome's enigmatic obsession for his record collection.

"Oh," replied Jerome noncommittally, not realizing he was about to be mentally vivasected by his host, without delicate employ of actual skinning knife.

"Yes, had a Victrola in the early days. Back at the bungalow. Got away from it. Out in the bush so much. Tried bringing the whole contraption out on safari for the evenings. Kept breaking things, turntable, needles. All that bouncing. Hardly practical."

"I see," replied Jerome, lost in his own thoughts.

"But I remember two selections I especially liked," reminisced Ernest, plowing ahead with conversation conducted largely with himself. Jerome wished Ernest would talk about the okapi instead and how unique to all he would be with those pictures.

"'In the Hall of the Mountain King' by Grieg and 'The Ride of the Valkyries' by Wagner. Those two stand out. They're supreme. Now, I've got a symphony of nature in the evenings." Ernest spread his arms while still seated, in a palm upward, evangelical manner and held them aloft sanctimoniously.

Jerome rapidly mumbled that it was nice that Ernest appreciated good music. He damned well wished Ernest would button up this music talk and tell him how well he had done on the first segment of their safari. Jerome had never heard of "The Ride of the Valkyries" or "In the Hall of the Mountain King," the two pieces Ernest had tallied among his favorites. Jerome hadn't the foggiest notion that both works appeared over a dozen times on various albums, home in his temperature-controlled vault.

The okapi was more shy than Ernest had expected. They scoured the thick undergrowth for days with no success. The other antelopes had been photographed along the long, grinding trail up to the forest lair, which now became their stern master. Jerome cursed the delay. The tentacles of vine switched his doughy face when he traipsed behind Ernest each day.

His evenings by the campfire became moaning complaint sessions. He soaked his feet in buckets of warm water heated by Ujiji and lamented the halcyon days just past, riding up in the Landrover, safely protruding through the roof vent, surveying his domain like an autocratic general inspecting columns of infantry troops standing at attention. Yet, his covetousness of those special okapi photos kept him from quitting altogether.

"We're doing all we can do," defended Ernest. "Remember, Westerners didn't even see one until 1900."

"I know, I know," snapped Jerome. "It's just that nobody, but nobody, anywhere around me at home has seen an okapi, maybe not in a blasted zoo even."

"That's a fair assessment, I'd say," allowed Ernest, studying searchingly his tormented client in the flickering light, through coils of ascending pipe smoke.

Four days more they treked. They had exasperating glimpses but nothing they could immortalize on film. That night in camp, Jerome fretted like a petulant child with an earache. Ernest nursed him with palaver.

"You got the big five and then all the antelopes on the way up here. Shots of the giant eland and the greater Kudu aren't as common as the Statue of Liberty postcards in New York drug stores! You realize that?"

Jerome was not easily soothed. The days were fleeting now. The gargantuan trawlers of earth movement were being readied with black, oily ointment at home. They were yawning, creaking, and stretching stiffly, man-rigged for their upcoming enslavement on the project.

"Maybe tomorrow," growled Jerome. "I'm going to bed."

The next day was miserable in the dense forests. Steady rain, beginning in midmorning, poured down through the layers of vegetation until by noon the entire party was sloshing to their lacerated knees in wet socks. No sightings were made. The rain subsided by evening and once again, in cooler air, Ernest and Jerome lounged in their canvas chairs with their drinks. Jerome was transformed. He was perky, gleefully childlike again as he had been weeks earlier on the easier, more comfortable part of the trip. Ernest couldn't fathom the change.

"I know what," summarized Jerome, applauding his chubby thighs with excitement.

"What's that?" ventured Ernest cautiously.

"If we run out of time and it looks like we might, you take them and send them later. Like they were mine. I - I mean I'll pay you much more of course. That's it! You're sending all the other shots after that fancy Nairobi studio does all that native frame stuff. It will work."

"But, but...," disallowed Ernest, hunching forward in his chair for emphasis, "how is it the same? I mean - mean, they won't be yours."

"No one will know. I have a private post office box. You can send them there, unframed. Air freight the frames over. I'll see they are matched up. I'll just wait after the first ones arrive, which we'll consign to the company address, until the okapi ones come. I'll buy time. Then, when I throw the viewing bash at the club, I'll just float them in."

Ernest deferred further debate and sagged limply back in his canvas chair. Jerome wouldn't understand. It wasn't the chase at all. It was the final result. He should have known. Carl was finally vindicated. Early the next morning, Ernest attacked the okapi pursuit with possessed vigor. He loathed the thought of being Jerome's clone after his departure even though the extra remuneration would mean that he wouldn't have to coax and cajole for several more weeks some new, rich American bore.

Jerome had made his peace with his new solution. Heretofore, always at Ernest's heels on the okapi quest, even while swearing and whining, Jerome now lagged back, dawdling with Ujiji and the porters. Hushed quiet by Ernest for their forest stalking, Jerome previously had remembered well, but now he joked freely along the queue. Ernest now knew that those pictures would be his alone to retrieve. By mid-afternoon, Ernest capitulated and halted their wanderings. Their bulletless rifles had been mentally stacked for the duration of the safari.

Champagne is traditional the last night out and so it was for them. Ujiji set the finest banquet of their entire camera safari, now well over a month in length. Jerome was ebullient. He divorced the elusive okapi from his mind. He had bought his okapi. He had seen to it.

Ernest labored through listening to all of Jerome's recent camera encounters. The jolting bump of the rhino, the dangling, rigid legs of the leopard kill, stiff as sounding pipes radiating from a bagpipe, the startle of the Cape buffalo, encountered point-blank among the bushes at the creek edge, all were rehashed by Jerome with the vacant interest of a violin recital held for a seven-year old, with no prospect of future talent.

Uncontentedly, Ernest puffed his pipe, clamping the stem with tensed cheek muscles. He should have been happy. On the drive back before the last camp, Jerome had scrawled a check, an amount in five figures, and had stuffed it folded, into the breast pocket of Ernest's bush jacket. He would not need another charter for nearly two months with the generous okapi advance.

He would have those shots in two weeks or less, without the impediment of Jerome thrashing about. The assignment would be short work. He would camp in the thickets with just Ujiji, forgo the protocol of evening campsites and be out with those pictures with alacrity. Just perhaps, if he were quick, fortunate, and able to muzzle Ujiji to secrecy with a sideward gift to him of a small part of Jerome's generous okapi advance, he could pull off his charade without the embarrassing episode ever reaching Nairobi. Still, he was unsettled. Never in his career had he been a surrogate photographer.

For all assembled, cross-legged, ground-sitting porters and Ernest imprisoned in his canvas throne, grandiose Jerome recited his self-proclaimed bravery well into the night. And then finally, mercifully, he yawned with the champagne and the foot-tramp of several days merging wearily together in fatigue. He rose slowly, unfolded stagily, and groaned audibly.

"Remember now, those okapi ones at my private box. Don't send them to my office. I'll float them in my way."

Ernest said nothing. Always he had been hopeful that duplicity would never be his longsuit, but he feared now that he held an ugly doubleton or at least a lonely singleton in his hand, perhaps one queen sporting an enigmatic Mona Lisa smile, that spoke directly to his great fear.

"Tell you what,' urged Jerome, standing about them now, erect, rotating his booze-laced neck painfully, before stumbling off to his tent.

"What?" deadpanned Ernest, realizing he must react in some manner.

"You deliver for me and I'll ship you a new stereo outfit. Better than any old Victrola. And, the best rendition money can buy of your...your...your 'Hall of the Val..Val..Valkrees' and 'The Ride of the Mountain King.'"

"'Hall of the Mountain King' and 'Ride of the Valkyries'," corrected Ernest with unmasked, bold irritation purpling his ambivalent countenance. His pipe slipped from his mouth and burned a bare knee before it was corraled in the flickering light from doing further damage.

106

"Whatever," returned Jerome over his shoulder, failing to decipher Ernest's annoyance, as he faded away, outside the circumference of the low campfire glow.

"They're yours. Your favorite songs, or whatever! Just get me an okapi," he called back from his tent flap.

Jerome's check, still folded in Ernest's pocket smoldered, hot now as a mustard plaster, hot as his pipe, and it branded his chest figuratively with ignominy. Well off, the solitary laugh of a hyena ate a piece of the darkness.

THE WALKING MAN

If it were important to notice, one could observe him step off the country road abruptly at the railroad crossing on his return each afternoon and then, balancing a brown sack of groceries in the crook of one arm, one could watch him make his way bumpily over the awkward spacing of black plank ties, until he disappeared toward his humble abode, a clapboard hut in a distant stand of unpainted shanties, all of which sighed with doddering age, down the tracks, a quarter of a mile from the country road, just where the ironhorse path curved from view.

If it were not important to notice, one scarcely would recognize the predictable pattern that had become his daily walking ritual. Varying through the year only by clock time, as man in his infinite wisdom had come to tinker with the sun each Spring and Fall, his walk up the country road, accompanying the natural peeking of early sun in the east, ushered in the dawn of each new day as the plumed rooster struts his barnyard domain at pink-fingered, first hint of morning light.

Always he walked protectively, defensively, on the shoulder of the narrow road, several feet off the pavement, as poking tentacles of civilization in recent years had nudged out to the country, choking now the long-forgotten road with the frightful morning bustle of coffee-laced, consumptive men and women, motoring early from their lavish, exurbanite cocoons to catch that edge for the day at their city centers of influence.

He interchanged two pair of walking shorts throughout the year. One was a tan canvas; the other, his favorite, was fray-ending, blotchy denim, a stringy, tussled survivor of many washing wars. In the very cold weather, during the brief southern winters, he reluctantly wore a pair of long pants. This pair, also distressed from wear, was newer than the two pair of shorts. The weather had to be quite cold for him to stoically select this calf-covering, full-length variety of trousers.

He was more opulent, however, with his ownership of shirts. He owned three: work-bleached blue; sweat-circled

111

brown; and dreary gunboat gray. Sockless always, the same rubber, low-quartered shoes, run over and run down, shod his bare feet every month of the year.

Hats were his most distinguishing feature. Unlike his extravagant choice of three possible shirts, the hat category numbered only two again to match his frugal collection of walking shorts. Easily his favorite was the chalk-white, metal construction hat. Resembling a Frank Buck jungle pith helmet, though not quite as domed, it rested squarely and stiffly atop his head, well down almost to his eyes, shading and obscuring much of his time-traveled face. It boasted breathing portholes, evenly spaced around, like tiny windows on a flying saucer. Perhaps a tenth of the time, he would treat any interested onlooker to a parade of his other hat. Jet black and short visored, this felt cap was a hybrid of beret and jaunty skimmer, much like the one worn by the repairman in the television commercials depicting the early, pioneer days of air conditioning maintenance.

Leaving his hidden hovel beyond the railway curve, his arms swung freely along the seven-mile hike up the country road to the great baronial estate where he worked each day. As he strode along with a proud, purposeful gait that would have become any man half his seventy years, he clutched, in one swinging hand, his noon repast of one gummy sandwich surrounded by waxed paper, and a tightly folded, plastic wad of crinkled raincoat.

Occasionally, on sun-drenched winter days, during the months of respite from the afternoon grumble of summer thunderstorm worry, he could be seen carrying nothing at all. Even his sparse sandwich was conspicuously absent from his grasp on those days. To a curious passerby, who noticed this rare absence of sandwich and raincoat, conjured visions formed of those shady noon hours spent sitting at the rear steps of the great home, feasting on slabs of gravy-running meatloaf, perhaps a butter-swimming boat of Idaho potato, and possibly a tiered pyramid of German chocolate cake, prepared and passed outside to him by the cook of the manor.

On his twice-a-day journeys, never did he socialize with passing traffic. In this, he did not discharge an air of haughtiness, only one of quiet privacy and independence. His gaze was ever downward, just ahead of his step, oblivious to the whooshing whisk of autos, zipping past only a few feet away from him. With his head ever inclined toward the ground, he searched for lost coinage or any other baubles of value. Stooping from the waist, deftly and quickly, he would appropriate any overlooked, glinty article of remote worth and give it a new home in his pocket. He would then be on his way again, briskly, without breaking his stride.

He selected the best routes for collecting as he went, those most likely to attract foot travel, and therefore most likely to experience dropped coin frequency. He would hastily cross and then cross again the country road to follow the newly emerging sidewalk paths, not for easier traipsing, as he was hearty indeed for rustic walking, but rather to heighten his chances of finding a forlorn dime or quarter, lying in wait for a new owner. Partial strips of sidewalk now ribboned much of his route. These fresh sidewalks snaked along in places, like spaced hyphens in a line, bordering the domain of their masters with the new subdivisions hidden behind them, sequestered beyond stout, brick walls that imprisoned each advertised uniqueness of special dwelling allure from the busy, passing plebeian world outside, from whence each subdivision would condescend to slurp its sustenance.

At one point, his hike took him past a bustling school. There he slowed each day, ever noticeably, realizing the loose sand there by the road held a great probability of sun-flashed metal. Somewhere, hidden under a bush on along a fence near the large, new supermarket on his way, he kept a secret cache of returnable bottles, which he would collect each afternoon on his return trip from his yard and handyman duties at the manicured estate. After retrieving them each afternoon from their grassy nest, he would insert the end digits of fingers into the necks of the bottles and would cart as many as three in one hand for deposit redemption at the supermarket counter. He purchased groceries almost daily at this classy emporium which had mushroomed into being as the large jewel in a necklace of smart shops along the country road, when the meteoric rush of cluster country living, now dotting the once pastoral landscape, demanded close neighborhood shopping. Rarely, did he wend home in the late afternoon without a tidy, brown sack of foodstuffs pinioned against his body.

A stolen glimpse inside any such container for a hasty survey of his comestible selections would have been enchanting indeed. The contents were never revealed but undoubtedly they numbered milk, bread, fresh meat, and leafy vegetables. Somehow he couldn't be envisioned as cluttering up any sack with swirly pastry, delicatessan goose liver, or strawberry daiquiri mix.

*　　*　　*

Near the fancy estate homes, where the walking man worked, but only on their periphery, in the older, more modest section of the rambling development, which had borrowed its name from the old country road Indian name itself, lived a man of curious ilk, a man who had become quite intrigued by the walking man.

From his auto, as they passed each other over the years, he had tried to acknowledge the walking man with a friendly wave. Time after time, all attempted greetings had been stymied by the ground slant angle of the walking man's concentration, as he scanned before him for coins and bottles. The development man had grown exasperated with his inability to communicate with this daily traveler of the road.

So, persistent to a fault, after many frustrating months, he resorted to beeping his horn at him. That tactic worked. Finally, the helmeted, engrossed walking man came to recognize the distinctive beeping and he would look up snatchily, instantaneously, without a hand greeting, for a fleeting peek at the direction of the sound and then he would return hurriedly to his monastic, bowed solitude in walking.

114

The development man was pleased that he had chosen to pursue this acquaintanceship, devoid of formal introduction. He felt he had bridged the gap to familiarity with him, unlike any other passerby, among the hundreds who passed by him each day.

Being enigmatic himself was perhaps the reason the development man was lured to the mystery of the walking man. He lived in the swanky development, though not among the very rich, and, like many of them, worked routinely in the city in a sedate, neat office in a quasi-professional job and, like many of them, he was a college bred man, but he was always fascinated by solitude, quietude, and oneness with himself. Hence, he was enchanted by the bold singularity and apparent insularity of the walking man.

As a very young youth, he had labored hard on the steaming trucks of a family business from age twelve until early adulthood and he had never forgotten the snooty smugness of many of their customers, unspokenly labeling the laborers as second class citizenry. He had always seized every opportunity as a young boy to converse with customers to show them that he wasn't some dim-witted dullard. When he spoke with them, he would chortle inwardly with satisfaction as their faces fell apart when they gave the obvious impression that this kid would be going places and that he wouldn't be stuck on a truck for long.

So, now in mid-life, reasonably successful to the limitation he allowed for himself in the senseless, mad scramble of the establishment world, he came to champion the common laborer. At fancy gatherings and parties, he usually wandered to one side, away from the knot of chattering din, and, when eventually missed, could be retrieved later from a sports trivia bout with a bartender, or from a huddle with some custodian who, with rollicking laughter, wavily clung to a broom for support, in tummy recovery from a bandy of juicy stories.

At his office, he often rapped with the maintenance people who wandered by on their rounds and when some royal princeling would flit down the arcade by his office, he would extract a belly-trembling laugh from them in remarking, "Duck, maybe he won't see us. Maybe his audience is with some other lucky soul in the building." In his business, he preferred the blue collar customer to the white collar variety. White collars show their dirty rings more readily, he always loved to say.

He was no saint, this development man, no shining example savior, even given his concern for all abused souls. No, not at all was he, despite his real interest in putting at ease ones whom he deemed less fortunate that he, through the offered little trinkets of kind words. He always had appreciated as a boy that cold pitcher of iced tea or that sprung-top bottle of pop offered quite infrequently then to him and his fellow truck laborers.

At his home in the development, twice a week in the dark, expressly for the garbage man, he left beer out at the street, along with the obvious barrels of trash. He would ice the beer down in a little pail, clattering its preparation outside in the black stillness of early morning and then, when the shuddering, massive truck squealed to a halt by his home at first dawn, he would nose a peek through a parted living room curtain to make certain that his little present had been claimed.

So, this self-styled philanthropist set about to win over the walking man. He never wanted to become overly chummy with him, just appreciated and understood. He wanted a distant buddy with whom he could share a nicety, a subtlety, a stolen, passing moment each day to and from his stuffy, starchy business life.

After the episodic horn ploy which signaled, only to the development man, an obvious, major breakthrough in their unilateral communication, he began to keep loose change on the dash of his auto and after days of vacillating uncertainty he launched his next bold act. When the walking man came into view, he would hastily roll down his driver side window and, without slowing down, driving rodeo style with one hand on the wheel, he began to lob shiny quarters or dimes in his direction. He tried to gauge his toss to have the coins plop in the loose sand or on a sidewalk just in front of his stride in order to maximize discovery possibilities.

This was no easy task, especially in the morning when traffic was heaviest, with its grousing bumper-riding compactness. In the evenings, with the migrations spaced over a longer period of return, he had a little more time to madly crank down his window. But, to his chagrin, the walking man, at first, displayed no reaction whatsoever toward any of the metal projectiles whizzing his way, launched by his unknown, officious benefactor. In his rearview mirror, the development man noted no hesitation in his step and no stooping to fetch any of the gifts. He was perplexed. Could it be that his coins were lightly plopping and settling in cushions of grass or lost in beds of sandy granules?

Sporadically, for several weeks, this practice continued, not at every passing but at most of them. Very occasionally, after some toss of coin, he would see the walking man startle a trifle to something apparently alien landing near him. Sometimes, when he sped away, treadmilled in moving traffic always, as the walking man shrunk from view, he would see him stop fully and glance about himself as if he were experiencing a strange happening he couldn't quite fathom.

As time progressed, it became maddening to the development man that his well-intentioned dimes and quarters were not being recovered, let alone appreciated. The development man rose to the occasion, reveled in its challenge, and became obsessed with success for his endeavor. He replayed in his mind his black spade, his ace of aces, journeyed by mind flight to the court of King Arthur to borrow Excalibur and mentally scrambled with bleeding knees and panting heart up countless mountain steps at the roof of the world for a solution bequest from the Dalai Lama himself.

Yes, he added as his final masterpiece, his crowning achievement, with as much class as a one-night carnival in a milltown, a blaring blast of horn with every windmilling toss of coinage from his driver window. After all, he rationalized,

117

he had honked his horn to first swivel the gaze of the walking man, so why not use the same method in bringing attention to his loose change munificence for him.

The walking man also initiated a new behavioral trend. He looked up more at passing autos as he walked. The development man wasn't positive but he concluded that his new trend of looking up must have stemmed from this newly discovered bounty of coin heralded by the ingenious addition of horn blast. Soon, it became obvious that the walking man had, indeed, come to associate his own passing auto with the catapulting projectiles of money. But the walking man always looked away when he saw his auto approach. "He's shy, the poor man, shy, and doesn't know how to thank me," concluded the development man. "He doesn't know how to show appreciation like the garbage men do with their waving salutes and broad, toothy smiles."

Then, shortly thereafter, their actual meeting, which had never taken place all those years on the country road, finally occurred late one afternoon at the supermarket. The development man had entered the supermarket for a few incidental items and exiting there, by chance, was the walking man with his little sack of daily groceries. They were upon one another without warning, in that slender funnel area in the front of the market, between interlocking rows of grocery carts and the squad line of rattling cash registers.

The development man tingled with anticipation, peacocking with pride, awaiting the effusion of glowing praise this walking man would somehow humbly stumble out in his direction in an attempted tribute for all he had done for him.

The development man spoke first, nervously fingering the knot of his loosened tie at his throat. "Hi! I...I guess you know who...who I am...I mean, I'm the guy who throws..."

A metal chain curtain descended with a clash of cymbal. The Berlin wall bullied through the front of the supermarket between them. "Yes, certainly, the walking man interjected with vivasecting dagger, "your antics would go unnoticed only to a blind man and sir, even in that elusive circumstance, you

118

would find a way I'm quite sure of attempting to reach that poor soul with whatever it is you need to accomplish and assuage for yourself."

The development man rocked back, shocked and dismayed, his whole life raced off a slack, celluloid reel, spinning wildly in an instant before him, exposing his folly before the world. Speechlessly, he tried to summon a reply but the walking man was already gone, striding proudly across the gleaming tile floor and then passing through the electronic doors, which had sensored to a purring parting for him as they would before a triumphant king who had just addressed his multitude of followers.

The development man's perspiration, welling clammily at every pore and bathed colder by the icy supermarket, made him shiver. His dress shirt clung to the small of his back. "Oh, no!" he blurted to himself. "His diction was that of, well, he sounded like Sir Laurence Olivier. So polished, so refined. Awful, you stupid fool!!" The development man patted his unruly, thinning hair down across his forehead and haphazardly felt his cheek, checking to see if he needed a shave.

Metal carts, piloted by shoppers with grocery lists, were backing up behind him as he was still standing where their first meeting had occurred. He moved finally, allowing the stream to pass.

"I bet he reads the classics. Hell, he must. Greek and Latin, maybe! His diction, wow!"

He wandered off down an aisle, not really choosing anything but afraid to venture out into the bright parking lot for fear of encountering the walking man so soon after their hallmark first meeting. He wasn't ready for that.

He sampled some free cold cuts displayed at the deli counter and finally selected a quart jar of apple juice from a shelf for his daughter. Then, dragging himself to the checkout line, he peered furtively outside through the glass, prayerfully hopeful that the walking man was not lurking outside waiting to devour him whole again with some poignant, deserving statement about himself. He didn't really expect to see him.

119

He really knew that he would be striding down the country road toward his secret home. He had far too much class to clobber him again, his opening skillful thrust had been lethal enough.

At the first opportunity, an early morning hour later in the same week, the development man, awash with guilt for days, activated his little speech which he had labored over pitifully, with as much agony as a shy, bookwormish valedictorian labors, delivering that graduation address they always feared they would one day have to present before snickering classmates and rump-rustling parents. He had recited it in the mirror shaving, and while watching television, deaf to persistent questions put to him by perplexed family members.

As the walking man approached him that morning, he pulled swiftly off onto a lumpy shoulder of road and with pumping hand raced the foggy window down into disappearance. The walking man stopped and turned resolutely to face him a few feet away across the road. Mutely, with shoulders hunched forward in an expectant battle stance of readiness, the walking man bristled defensively.

"I owe you a sincere, sincere apology. I truly hope that you will accept it," said the development man, with quaking timbre in his voice.

With a loose hand gesturing skyward, conducting a single pacifying index finger, the walking man silently managed an omniscient, faint smile and replied wordlessly, with his metal helmet speaking forgiveness in the form of a stiff nod in the direction of the development man. Then he was off again, pivoting his rubber shoes slippingly in the soft sand. In his hand, between his wrapped, gummy sandwich and his crinkled, folded plastic raincoat, was a wafer-thin, calf-bound book, richly bordered wine-red, and styled with gold leaf embroidery.

Poems? Essays? Strange, the development man thought. He had never noticed a book before, so quick had been their passings, so brief their encounters, and so evident that part alone, which he had chosen to see.

PERSPECTIVE

"But I got all the golf balls, every one to be gotten," defended Harry, hoisting himself up from an inclined position in his family room rocker.

"Here are some more," contradicted his son, Scooter, standing in the hall doorway before him with a blush of respectful grin shining across his face.

With a polite smirk, Scooter smugly opened one hand and displayed four golf balls in various stages of climate-distressed condition as contrary evidence to his father's assertion. They were quite useable, their skins were intact with no cutting smiles, and they were only a little rain-pelted with time, from their several month siesta, reposing on the vacant field behind their home.

"I can't believe it," repeated his father, opening his palms to display no hidden, rhetorical weapons of explanation. "I combed that field when you were away at school. C'mon, tell me where you got those four. Own up."

Harry awaited an explanation. None was forthcoming.

"You bought 'em?", he pressed.

"Nope!" replied his son. "You borrowed them from one of the guys?" "Nope!" pronounced his son, glowingly.

Scooter loved making his father squirm and fret. Harry was so monomaniacal about Scooter's future and that pro tennis career malarkey, always decreeing his broad wisdom as benefit of his vast experience in living, that Scooter couldn't help enjoying having him broil on a turning skewer once in a while. Scooter never was nasty about it, but it was a way of taking a small ounce of flesh back from the totalitarian adult world.

"I can't believe it," denied Harry, casting his head about the room, searching for a logical answer.

"The field?"

"Yes," frolicked Scooter.

"Our field?"

"Yes."

"You're sure?"

"Yes," laughed Scooter, collapsing back in a heap on the

family room sofa. He adjusted back down on his head his ball cap with the Greek fraternity letters emblazoned on the front, propped his splayed hands behind his head, and 'kicked back' as they said up at college, when one starts relaxing after some frenzied pace of class, library booking time, strenuous athletic workout, or a harmless girl-watching excursion of the mind in the school cafeteria.

He placed his huge, sneakered feet delicately up on the coffee table and smiled across at his father. He had been reminded of his big athletic hooves dirtying the coffee table so he was careful where he rested them.

"Now listen here, young man," began Harry, now sitting fully erect, with the footrest sprung into disappearance as now part of the rocker base. "When I reluctantly heard you were playing golf as a pressure release from the tennis season, I really started looking for golf balls on my evening walks on the field."

"I know, you wrote me you had a pile, kind of a mound of them building up on my bed."

"Right, I did. I looked for them only because you were ostensibly playing hard enough tennis to warrant a safe, occasional break from it." Harry always used a big word like 'ostensibly' around his son. It was part of his self-imposed wisdom lesson. Harry was always cutting out Word Power from the monthly Reader's Digest and putting that list of twenty vocabulary words squarely on his son's pillow.

"So," continued Harry, "remembering those shag balls flying on the field last year when that practice duffer was out flailing away on evenings when I took my walks, I figured I might just collect a few strays he had overlooked. For you, you see."

"Hey, I appreciate it," assured his son, "On a budget up at school, those balls will come in handy when we hack around."

"Make sure it is just that," snapped his father.

"Just what?" queried Scooter, squinching his eyes. No furrowing of loose skin folded across his quizzical forehead. He was too young for furrow definition. He would have to wait for that.

"You know what! You're a tennis player, on scholarship, that's what! You've got a world of talent, so just don't get too enamored with golf. No touch football. No frisbee throwing on even quiet streets. No grab ass around the fraternity. Protect yourself. You're the franchise for the whole team."

Harry was proud of his employ of the word 'enamored.' It would be another two weeks before the Reader's Digest would arrive. He would hardly be able to contain himself then with the excitement of clipping out the vocabulary list for edictal placement on Scooter's pillow. So 'enamored' would do for now.

Scooter settled further down into the cushioned sofa, realizing now it had been a mistake to sit down at all. He should have remained standing at the doorway. It was that time again. The frequent, melodramatic, floating soap-opera hour, when Harry pulpitized his own plan for Scooter's future, was about to begin, without relief of commercial interruption provided anywhere during the ordeal.

"Ghastly," murmured Scooter inaudibly. "Endure, endure and split as soon as possible," spun around unannounced in his brain. "He means well, stay and suffer, it won't last forever," he reassured himself, trapped in the family room.

Harry, in early evening, was already in his pajamas in the family room. He had finished a long walk on the field with again no further golf balls to his credit. Now, showered, with rumpled, uncombed hair, he was before the tube sports shrine for a early evening of viewing.

Harry took long walks on the field every third night, played hard, rigorous tennis every third night and, in further inviolate rotation, ran laps totaling a mile around his circular driveway every third night. It was twenty-one laps around his driveway to equal a mile run. Harry knew that for certain because he had driven his car around the driveway twenty-one times to gauge it. Harry wasn't loony, he just appeared loony. He had felt secure in driving the entire twenty-one laps instead of using simple multiplication after circling around his driveway only a few times. Harry was horrid at math, but he always clobbered those vocabulary tests in Reader's Digest.

"Are you practicing a lot?" explored Harry with the sombreness of a black-robed, juvenile judge.

"Sure, always do. My own pace. Running a lot, too."

Scooter glanced at the mantel over the fireplace to check the time. The antique clock had wound down to stony silence. He did know it wasn't 11:22 because his awakened stomach told him it was supper time. He was marooned now in the family room, awaiting supper being prepared by his mother in the adjoining kitchen. He would try one ploy which had worked before.

Harry was warming to his own Chautauqua, lathering himself for his congregation of one. He had edged up on the front of his rocker.

"Boy, can you hit it. And, that speed. They can't teach that speed, you know. Everything else, but they can't teach that speed." He knifed his points home on the merits of a pro tennis career with one stiff-fingered hand slamming into the reddening, open palm of the other.

"Ex...excuse me, just a second, Dad," interrupted Scooter, "Let...let me get something to drink, had a long bike workout."

"C'mon back," pleaded Harry, sighing back in his rocker.

Scooter bolted from the room in earth-gobbling strides. He dashed into the kitchen and poured a hissing, warm soda over cube-stacked ice, shaken down into a tall glass. Then, gingerly, he tiptoed beyond his father's aural range, to the nearby laundry room and quickly selected a towel from the clean pile his younger sister had folded neatly that day as part of her assigned, household chores.

In returning to his father's loving tirade, the towel would serve as body language, a subconscious sensor that meant he was listening, attentive with polite adolescent respect, but yet, as a subtle, hypnotic signal it was introduced, as certainly father he had somewhere to go, and soon, hopefully, he would be allowed to go there. Scooter then clopped back across the

126

kitchen floor, louder than before to herald his return. Unobtrusively, he folded the towel over one knee as he took his place on the sofa again. Strategically, he also selected a seat just a mite closer to the hall getaway door, and thusly, just a little closer to a shower and temporary freedom.

Fooled by Scooter's ploys, Harry was not without one of his own. When his son had left the room, Harry had unfolded himself laboriously from his rocker, lumbered across the room and, without entering the kitchen, had snaked a paw around the corner into the kitchen to dislodge the telephone receiver, eliminating the possible annoying chance of interruption from that source.

"Mind you, golf is fine in its place. That Swedish whiz, number four in the world, plays golf away from tennis. But, and there is a but young man, you are on scholarship! Make sure you are a self-starter and don't let things slide."

Scooter gazed mutely across the room, elbows pointed on his knees. That is, one elbow was directly on one knee; the other, on his folded towel, his only ticket for house lights and intermission.

"You know, your speed can't be taught," droned Harry with as much originality as a midnight congressional filibuster on Capitol Hill.

"They can teach everything else. You get your speed from your mother's side," he offered generously.

"If I died tomorrow..." This was the one that always took the proverbial cake. Scooter gulped and his ears burned. "If I died tomorrow, and there was no life insurance, which of course there is, you could, in six months, six months mind you, play the small tour and make it from necessity."

Harry was a life insurance salesman. This ploy of taking the father out of the picture was one of the oldest sales tools in his profession, taking the father and planting him, burying him, making the poor guy feel guilty during the sale presentation at the kitchen table in his own home with his wife and kids gathered around him. It wasn't a lie, only a gruesome reality that usually made a sale.

Scooter fidgeted with the towel on his knee and swiveled his head to gaze through the shadowy, black eye of their television. It was no diversion, mute and tunnel deep with space.

"Six months," Harry reiterated, "you know what they say about necessity."

"What?" deadpanned his son.

"Necessity is the mother of invention." Sometimes Harry offered little epigrams and famous sayings in addition to vocabulary words for Scooter's edification.

"Don't grow up too fast. You work forty years, no matter. Surgeon, scientist, businessman, uh, taxicab driver. No different. Don't let your youth go. Don't try to hurry out where your Mom and me are. It doesn't get a whole lot better in the business world, believe me."

Harry slumped back in his chair, spent with broken-record repetition, panting in an effort to collect himself for a dynamic summation.

Scooter stretched his long arms out before him, yawned decorously and, from his seated position near the breakaway hall door, strategically moved his towel to the knee farthest from Harry for another tactical pawn move in his favor.

Scooter knew his father loved him and he knew why he made him endure all these hype lectures. He knew you only had to worry about people not caring, when they stopped talking about you. Scooter knew he was a great talent but good enough to make a living with a pro tennis career was debatable, even with total dedication. He could appreciate his father's vicarious dream, seeing in him the blinding speed his father never had, coupled with the heady savvy for the game which admittedly his father did have for his own tennis game.

But his father just didn't realize that hundreds of bright hopefuls were dedicated to a pro playing career. Earlier, in the father's day, only a couple of dozen players at any one time entertained any such thought. Plus, he mused silently as his father gathered himself for another slide forward in his rocker for a benedictory salvo, many of those foreign players, now

128

from virtually every country in the world, were dedicated to the point of zombie enslavement to the game. If they failed on the pro circuit, and most would, they would be relegated to a lifetime of stringing racquets in the bowels of some club pro-shop or organizing beginning lesson sessions, year after year, for twenty foot-stamping, squealing tykes with their twenty gum-cracking, pushy mothers lined up at courtside, coaxing junior to glory when junior was in actuality only a cute, talentless brat. For these reasons, Scooter was most interested in keeping a dynamic academic career flourishing at college as well as displaying his athletic talents.

Harry swung the footrest down again with employ of handle and waddled to the end of his rocker. His massive chest scended through his open pajama top as a dockside boat rises and falls rhythmically with endless, slapping wash of wave.

Scooter looked deep into the abyss of the dark television. He wasn't annoyed, just bored and long-suffering in attentiveness. He damned well wished he could grab a shower and split to the fairly safe haven of his girl friend's house. However, he wasn't safe there. Periodically, Harry would call him there to remind him to do something which he had forgotten to tell him.

Harry tried a new approach. He switched gears. Perhaps his own sermons were sounding a little moldy to his own ear.

"Okay, own up, where did you get those four balls?"

Scooter appeared surprised that his father had suggested a recess from wisdom hostility class. He seized upon it.

"From the field. That place," he reassured with a devilish grin.

"Where there are no more balls. Where I got them all," Harry concluded with headmaster finality.

Scooter laughed and tugged at the visor of his cap. He really had his Dad on the griddle and it was warming nicely.

"Look, when I first noticed them, months ago, in the Spring, then in that ankle-high grass, I would come home with six, seven, even eight, as if that guy hitting those shag balls months ago was abducted by a UFO in mid-swing. I mean they were there. Must have been a rich guy because he didn't look too hard for those errant hook drives. Then, in time, the harvest dropped off. Three, two, one. I haven't found a golf ball in six weeks and you find four, those four in your hand. C'mon, gimme a break. Think I was born yesterday?"

"Yesterday morning," smirked Scooter. "I found them right there where you said," solemnized his son, after sneaking in his little dart on the very recent time of Harry's birth.

Harry stroked his five-o'clock cheek shadow at seven o'clock and shook his head, while pouching his lips with air. Scooter shuffled the golf balls adroitly in the cup of one strong hand.

"A hundred times in the last year. I walk that field with my trusty 5-iron walking stick for snakes, over the same area where I found the balls. I criss-cross that area coming from our house side, like cops in a line looking for a dead body. Haven't seen a ball in weeks. The seventy I put on your bed was the crop, I tell you."

Scooter tugged his ball cap down on his head, called through to his mother in the kitchen to inquire on the progress of dinner, and patted again the towel on his knee. He remained silent but he continued to smile slightly. He was beginning to enjoy himself but he still wanted a hasty retreat from the family room and the family minister.

Harry continued, playing out his scratchy record, the one slowed by the muddling, linty needle. "The only damn time I didn't walk over that area while up there was the time I drove up the dusty road and entered on the other side because your Mom wanted some bricks for a flower bed border and I had c-a-s-u-a-l-l-y remarked to your Mom at the time, that the construction men had discarded some nice bricks in a heap."

Scooter howled. He clapped his bare, muscular thighs below his tennis shorts with syncopated thwacks and sunk back laughing into the deep plushness of the sofa. In his excitement, his towel slipped to the floor.

"What's so funny?"

"Oh? Nothing, Dad, nothing," he said, continuing to laugh.

130

"What the hell is so funny?" pursued Harry curiously, rather than dictatorially. "Huh?" Harry waited for an explanation. "Well?"

"It's just that, well, uh the bricks, that's what," answered Scooter with grinning mystery.

"The bricks? The bricks are funny?"

"No! I mean, today when I got those four balls. The bricks..."

"You lost me. Riddles. Don't talk in riddles."

Scooter stood and stretched his lower back, grimacing subconsciously without pain. Years before he had experienced lower back pain during an important segment of his high school tennis career. The whole family routine had ground to a halt, so anticipatory was Harry's concern for Scooter's health and well-being, just for tennis of course, and then, secondarily, for life in general. Scooter had learned that phony grimacing with his back flung his authoritative father into a comical tailspin.

"Today. Mom asked me to see if I could get some more bricks for the backyard flower bed border. She told me about you driving up the dusty road before and getting them for the front flower bed. So, I did."

"So...?" befuddled Harry.

"So, while I was up there anyhow, I found the golf balls over that same area where you found the others before, in from that abandoned, rusty swing set landmark."

"No more balls on that field," declared Harry, wonderingly.

"I just parked, slung some bricks in the hatchback, and took a little walk on the field in from the brick heap," continued Scooter, still chuckling.

The phone jangled in the kitchen. His Mom had placed the receiver quietly back on the cradle minutes earlier. Scooter seized his leave.

"That's probably for me," he announced hopefully. He was already standing for the final anthem. Maybe his Dad would skip the benediction at the end, just this once, the one about dropping out of college if he couldn't decide on a major course

131

of study, coming home and eating off the family table for six months without paying board, living at home for six months without a job, training for a real chance at the tennis pro tour. He could just visualize it. His Dad would have white posterboard plastered all over the house, color coordinated with shaded calendar days for running, drilling, and even relaxing, a veritable battlefield of instructions, complete with nutrition and sleeping nonsense too.

"I'll get it. Got to hustle with a shower." Scooter galloped down the hall.

"Six months," Harry trailed feebly, after his escaping form.

The following day seemed endless, one of the longest in Harry's entire life. He paced agonizingly across his office like a new zoo animal, pressing his nose to the cold glass, watching the sheeting rain whip across his office parking lot. He searched the sky four times an hour seeking a patch of blue, one solitary patch of blue. Twice, distractively, he had dropped the receiver of his phone to the floor on incoming calls and had needed to apologize for battering the eardrums of clients calling in with juicy business orders to report.

The day crept along incalculably, a lifetime, then a century, as a condemned man hears gallow hammering from his cell, knowing the appointment early the next morning is with him. It really didn't matter if the rain stopped. Harry was going anyhow. He often walked in the rain on his field, even during lightning storms.

Finally his work day ended. A pearly, leaden sky, lighter now with a yellowing cast, signaled an end to the soaking rain. Harry dashed home, splashing his tires through small lakes of rain water which swam over roadbed curbing.

Madly he changed into his heavy walking gear; long sweat pants, and accompanying long-sleeve sweat shirt. In his haste, he couldn't get his left leg in the sausage-tight pant leg. He fumbled, then stumbled, and tripped over his bed, swearing to himself. He raised his left leg from a supine position where he had fallen and engineered it in that way up through the hugging, elastic-bottomed tourniquet of cloth.

132

He had been the first one home. Grabbing his ritualistic 5-iron walking stick, he made for the front door. But, this day he broke established routine. He didn't pad down the driveway, waddle through his backyard thicket, and cross the winding creek on the concrete bridge to his window of entry on his field, as he had done scores of other times.

He was taking the car this late afternoon. He hoped he wouldn't be seen. Slowly backing from his driveway, he eased up the hill behind his house, craning to select the right artery of side road that would empty near the hidden, dusty road that formed a quaint, country border to the large field behind the development. On the first sniff, the bloodhound nose of his machine selected the right entrance amid the maze of possible subdivision streets and he guided himself stealthily to a purring cease of engine alongside the pilfered cone of bricks, the large pile from which he had borrowed months ago, and the new smaller, broken pile from which Scooter allegedly had appropriated more border bricks for his mother the previous day.

Harry unfolded himself stiffly from his car and shut the driver door silently, as one does in a funeral queue upon arriving at graveside behind a hearse. The broad expanse of field always overwhelmed Harry with its rolling beauty. He cherished its closeness almost reverently when he came to unwind after a harrowing day at the office. But, he seemed to fumble this day with the secret, motoring entrance. He was much more familiar with his walking approach in from the other side.

Dawdling with hesitation, he petulantly kicked the drooping cone of brick, time damaged now across its sloping edge like the skin of the Pyramids and the noseless, wind-swept Sphinx. He was melancholic with ambivalence, and felt uneasy with the strangeness of the sensation. He should have felt confident and relaxed on his field, but somehow he was not, a faint weakness of uncertainty lurked within him.

He leaned against his car and gazed full into the afternoon sun, across the half-mile to the abandoned swing set which

133

formed the northern border of his previous golf ball harvest. He squinted his eyes in the glare and cupped a hand as a visor across his eyebrows. The sun, shining in his eyes, paroled again now from the dungeon of afternoon rain, made the field shimmer with miraging waves of illusion.

"Sure, stupid, the sun's always to your back when you walk in your way from the other side," Harry solved aloud to no one. Feeling better for his scientific theorem, Harry started off across the field. The sun glinted off the other blade side of his 5-iron walking stick, opposite the side that normally reflected late afternoon sun.

He couldn't remember the grass looking so yellow-green, sparkling in the sun, droplet wet from the recent downpour, unlike the normal vista swaying musically before him on other afternoons when the sun warmed his back instead of spotting his eyes. The summer, calf-high, grass grained toward him, nodding obeisance in a gentle breeze as he strode through it. Strange, he mused. From the other side he hadn't noticed before the angle of its growth.

He passed known landmarks without recognizing them. Large gopher holes, the pressed rut of jeep tires, the nasty clump of trash, the familiar plastic baby mattress with the sprung coil and receding circles of dried, innocent urine all were upon him before their usual salutes of greeting announced themselves at places of customary routine, as they had all the other late afternoons.

He paused, disoriented, and turned completely around, dizzily, asking for his bearings to return to him. He azimuthed a new path off a familiar knot of trees, to his right now, forever to his left before, and proceeded reassuredly with the approaching swing set again located through the glare and the wand-waving grass. The power lines overhead, distant to his right, comfortably left before, were an untouchable but comforting, visible tether to compassing sanity if everything else failed him.

Finally, he entered the zone, that ten thousand square foot patch of field that had been the landing area for those shagbag golf balls, that place he had picked clean as a bean field before a hurricane, with his methodical search for golf balls during Scooter's Spring term at college.

Harry was self-assured again. Familiarity breeds contempt. He swiveled completely around his grounded walking stick, orchestrating and enjoying established routine. He turned and turned, smugly, almost callously with cocky certainty.

"Ah," he remarked, "my field and not a golf ball left on your brow." Harry felt good and spoke to himself on his stage of field as a Shakespearean actor projects great truth from an Elizabethan theatre-in-the-round to a spellbound host of audience gathered below and about him.

He continued on through his unstaked preserve. His field was not posted; he was not trespassing. There, just before him, catching his eye, its contour silhouetted in the sun under a breeze-blown cover of grass, a jewel beckoned. What was it, perplexed Harry inwardly, a rock, a stone? Harry laid back its shelter of grass and exposed it to the world.

Dimpled and dirty, rung with a crest of wet sand from its view-top equator, a golf ball winked up at him. Dejectedly, he bent to acquire it, and defeatedly, with numb, rote movement, he cleaned it with thumb and forefinger and with a rubbing slide up his smelly pant leg, before sequestering it in his shorts pocket, beneath his heavy pants.

He slunk on, dragging his 5-iron walking stick, sullenly ribboning his telltale discovery voyage behind him weavily in the wet grass.

Another field jewel twinkled. Harry closed his eyes. It smiled mockingly up to him, from its camouflaged position under a bush he had passed a hundred times from the other side.

Salty tears mixed with perspiration welled up in the corners of Harry's burning eyes but they abdicated swiftly in favor of the broad smile which stole resignedly across his face.

"Damn kid. So be a big success in business."

135

THE IMPOSSIBLE DREAM

Hours earlier practically all fluids had spilled from his body, streaming out his pores like water gushing from a tilted watering can. Now, mustering supreme effort, Don, in early afternoon, lower in spirit that a crawling serpent's navel, was shaving and showering, after having slumped alone, for an agonizing hour, in the lonely cloister of his bedroom, where he had fought desperately to collect shattered shards of fragile ego from the aftermath of the Florida morning tennis match, which had been dueled unsuccessfully, outdoors in the blistering August cauldron of battle.

Don had not wanted to go anywhere. He would have been quite content just to sit and drink and fume over the defeat of that morning but thankfully he knew that would be a mistake as the wound of disappointement, tinctured with false, ineffective, alcoholic placebo would only erupt later in greater unhappiness as some hideous, disfiguring rash of the mind. So, he got himself going somehow, feigned a good attitude to the other three members of his family, dressed grumpily and numbly readied himself to surprise his wife at her performance that afternoon.

Don's son, his partner in defeat at the morning match, also was to attend the performance. He would be driving his own car and taking his girlfriend. While Don banged around his own room, grousing to himself, trussing himself into a stiff white shirt and cinching necktie on the cloudless, stove-hot afternoon, his son dressed in his own room, orderly and placidly, with no apparent disspirited residue from the morning match. At least, Don couldn't detect any outward disappointment. But perhaps,he reasoned, his son might be hiding his hurt as he was attempting to mask his own bitter sorrow. His son left before Don to collect his date.

Don left for the theatre with just enough time allotted for him to make the curtain. He hated going places and waiting once he arrived. Over the years, in conducting business without the aid of wristwatch, he had become a veritable master in estimating time when time mattered. When time wasn't important, Don was usually late. Don never wore a wristwatch, claimimg his condition of high blood pressure made any constraints of his wrist painful and uncomfortable.

Don's auto was a steam cabinet of stale, torrid air. As companion for the ten-mile drive to the college theatre, washing in three trays of cracked ice, Don had constructed a quart-size tumbler of dark brown bourbon and water, his faithful enemy for driving whenever he ventured out, penguined uncomfortably in snazzy duds for special places like the theatre. He deserved it, he rationalized narrowly, what the hell, he had been good, abstinent for several days, readying himself for the match and they had lost. Touche' body, he repined privately, I coddled you and you let me down, so I'll punish you now with drink.

Don rationalized everything around a fulcrum of booze. He was comical in earning his drinks. Now, in early middle age, he would jog in the hot summertime in a prison of heavy clothes and plod about his lawn, mowing grass in long, black sweat pants when everyone else puttered about in bathing suits. Mentally, he sweated his way to another liquid reward. Don wasn't a bad sort, talented really in a myriad of fields with that broad, brush stroke dilettantism which made for enlightened, good conversation and confusing, fashionable wonder but which, alas, usually wanted for substantive credentials with any final analysis.

Named for a famous, silent screen heroine, the quaint, tasteful college theater had been a landmark in the community for decades. As a small boy in the years following World War II, Don had been brought there with his parents to view college plays. The theater then, as he recalled, was different, not as elegant as in its present, refurbished state but darkly and magnificently medieval somehow, like the vaulted, torch-lit banquet hall of a Norse king.

With a generous bequest from a wealthy alumnus, the theater had been renovated recently. It now boasted plush, red-cushioned seating, a sumptuous foyer, excellent restrooms, and most importantly, adequate backstage dressing rooms. Some rococo markings, a garnish of cream-white statuettes, and the original ornate ceiling remained as an architectural reminder to its heritage.

Heretofore, the community had been embarrassed when the nationally acclaimed theatrical intelligentsia had graced the college town with visiting performances, but now, with the face lifting, the theater needed to apologize no longer and culturally too, none of its proud enchantment had been forfeited.

Don's wife, necessitiously now a successful career woman with Don's carousel excursions in various careers demanding two income stability, loved singing and acting. And, she was good at her new avocational craft, truly good. She had scurried back to people and essential diversion beyond her homelife, without neglecting family in the process once she had become convinced that Don with certainty was cordoning people off from himself, for the foreseeable future.

It frightened her to be so sequestered, mentally grazed with a tether rope, with just Don and his new recoiling, hermetic ways, hiding behind the bottle and his own sad, twenty-year short circuitry in three business careers. She loved him and would stay with him, but she damned well was not going to be like him. Don understood and now encouraged her periodic theatrical productions and the accompanying night practices, as it afforded him more time alone in which to pursue his dabbling excursions in daydreaming, writing, reading, and general, lofty reflections on the state of all things, real and imagined.

The play was a musical adaptation of one of the great works of literature, an opera based on the conflict between dis-illusion and hope, dream and reality, that monument of seventeenth century Spanish literature, with the hero tilting at windmills, from which emerges today that spelling bee and crossword puzzle teaser, "quixotic", meaning the pursuit of imaginary, lofty, romantic ideals.

The repertory group, valiant, everyday career people with fulltime jobs, had practiced for weeks, well into each night, after their taxing, daily work routines. They were embarking this weekend on the seemingly impossible, Herculean task of staging fourteen performances over the ensuing two weeks. Don's wife had been glowing for weeks. Diligently she had attended every practice without complaining and she, through it all, had not shirked any of her career or household callings. With a boundless reservoir of energy, she had hummed her lines liltingly, while bustling tirelessly at her office and at her home. Her appetite for the added challenge made Don jealous and weary.

Now, Don was no bum, no, not at all, thank you very much. Sedulously, he went to his office every day and punched out the paperwork blizzard required in his job. He even pursued new accounts occasionally and, although his performance could never be called academy award material, he was able sometimes to manage a meek nod of approval to a chameleon-shaded establishment lie when it was job-safety expedient to play out a business charade.

He was conservative, a modest consumptive type, and he lived frugally, unlike the prodigal, leaky money days of his early marriage years. He never went to bars anymore. He loathed bars and he never stayed out late. Most early evenings, he could be found already home, lumbering through a nap which preceded a long walk or a spirited jog.

Don never could figure out what made him so tired all the time. Whenever he went to the doctor expecting a bad report, the report never was too bad. Don was almost disappointed. If he were legitimately sick, then his tiredness would be justified. He felt guilty about his tiredness and constant, drooping fatigue. He had read all the stress journals, and there he was, in living color, the unmistakable archetype of stress---stumble weariness, slightly overweight, too much alcohol, deep unhappiness with his career, the discarder of old relationships---bold print, chapter headings, every one.

Thank God he didn't smoke. Certainly, with that added vice, he already would have had a mildewing tombstone dedicated in his name. Maybe it was simply him. He had had only three jobs in over twenty years so he couldn't be accused of job instability. But it was there, indelibly, the deep insecurity, the deep fear, the pressing unhappiness, the sales career remaining, without the self-selling esteem and vigor.

His wife would break out periodically in hives worrying about him. He was an enigma. He had so much talent and it would surface over and over again, and everyone would cluster, tense with anticipation, frozen with rapt interest, holding their breaths, waiting for Don to zoom to the zenith of his potential, but it would never happen. Like the home team titillating the crowd by loading the bases with no outs in the ninth inning, only to fail to score in order to win the game, Don's crowd about him would grumble and mutter with mingled notions of wonder, surprise, and disgust and then they would ultimately disband and trudge off quietly, leaving Don alone.

He wasn't a bum and whatever Don really was, he certainly wasn't stupid either. He sensed all these things about him. While at home in the evenings, sipping poison, gratefully controlled more and more now as he aged, he was aware. He just didn't want in on the maddening big race anymore. He chose little races, off main betting tracks. He had been a contestant for years earlier in life, in the big race, and now, he had come to hate that event. All relationships he now eventually found tawdry, vapid, and stale. He never felt the world owed him anything and he wasn't down on people spitefully, he was too cheerful generally for that hollow agony, but he just never came to believe in anything.

That was his problem. He had tried to believe in people and things but each time when he was poised vulnerably, prickled with excitement over some person or thing that everyone about him deemed so passionately dear, and indispensable for well-being, Don would find out the truth about that person or thing, that horrible, sunlight-naked truth, that the real embodiment of their pandering quest was no better than his individual embodiment itself, and then therefore really not worth any special prostrated pursuit on the part of anyone.

So, he just simply punched his time card, in and out,

143

perfunctorily, at the factory of human interaction. He still helped sweet old ladies across busy streets and he still patted the curly heads of little tykes with a grin and kind word, but beyond that, he was gone. The gregarious, vortical center of activity around people that had typified his early adult life, orchestrated then perhaps too boisterously and agitatedly, was no longer to be found anywhere. He had been desperate for friends as a young man, covetous and seeking, agonizing over not being universally liked, and now, he eschewed all friendships as being unfit to satisfy the very definition of the word, and tolerated only superficial acquaintanceships.

Don arrived at the theatre on the dot of reported curtain rise. The curtain had been held however, to allow the sparse, predominantly senior citizen Sunday crowd to cautiously thread its way down to seats. His son and date were already seated across the theatre, up front near the orchestra pit, where they could receive a good view of the thespian mother. Don met their gaze, and it was offered back to him broadly, spontaneously with happiness, and again, as earlier at home, he could not ascertain one, solitary mote of disappointment on his son's face as leftover memory from their tennis defeat that morning.

Sighing deeply, Don plopped into his plush seat, content to be stationary and immobile. The house lights were dim but steady, not yet flickering. Don loved dark places. Dark places hid dirt and clutter and reality. The theatre, with its token little balcony, had room for almost four hundred people but only eighty seats were needed this Sunday. Don had attended many of these repertory musical productions before, supportive to his wife, and they were good, genuinely professional, and yet, there were always rows of empty seats. The productions failed to draw the community attendance they deserved.

From their sunken pit, with white heads barely visible at floor level, the tidy, six-piece orchestra was tuning quietly, quite unlike the frenzied loosening up of a large, complete orchestra with its discordant cacophony of many intruments. Don glanced about him in the gloom during those final few

144

minutes before the beginning of the performance. So antipodal in serenity and repose was the little theatre, filling slowly with its well-behaved, library-hushed, knots of people from the raucous, straining, grunting tennis court of battle he had experienced a few hours earlier.

Dear old ladies with neat, blue coiffures and thick, plain eyeglasses, toddled down the sloping aisles in stiff, black shoes, tasteless with design, and they gingerly finger-tested their shuffle by touching the backs of seats as they balanced themselves along their way, while acclimating their sightworn eyes in the mechanical rosepink twilight of early afternoon.

Most of them were conspicuously without husbands, widows undoubtedly, having outlived their respective men, practically to a woman. With warming blood circulation slowed by age, they carried sweaters or wore shawls across their bony, slight shoulders, despite the incongruity of the calendar. Don nodded courteously when they chanced near his seat and they twinkled cherubic smiles in return when they bumped close enough to distinguish his shadowy image. They all clustered in the front near the orchestra pit, in slender rows for mutual protection, as there, fading eyesight would have every advantage during the performance.

The young, energetic college crowd, proper and refined, chic with arty, snooty urbanity, eclectic in apparel with a displaced wardrobe gamut from washer-distressed bluejeans to penguin-starched tuxedoes, sat together at the rear, in a closer commune than even the dear old ladies formed at the front. They bunched in cliques and did not form long, slender rows for mutual defense. They spoke quietly, with giggling interspersion, earnestly, with heads inclined together with that animated, gossipy wonder reserved for the whirl of late adolescence.

Between the two age groupings, in the center of the theatre, rows of empty, red-upholstered seats waited patiently for patrons who would not come. And, with their vacancy, a sharp contrast occurred to Don. There was an evident paucity of middle-aged people in the theatre. The old and young were

145

sequestered rigidly by choice to themselves and the sea of empty middle seats between them demarcated the difference of mood between the two generations.

The house lights flickered and faded. Don hoped that mercifully, a calming transformation from the agony of the morning match would be complete with a plunging immersion into the performance. And, it did not disappoint him. The performance was thrilling. Don sat close enough to the stage to see the vivid rapture glowing on their faces, to experience the full-bodied, melodic singing in the most earthy way of seeing uncontrolled saliva occasionally fly from their round mouths when they projected lustily and vigorously their passionate notes.

Early in the first act, Don's wife, center stage and terrific, able only to detect forms in the darkened crowd through the blinding, scorching stage lights, fuzzily spotted his faceless, white shirt. Don knew she had seen him. It made him feel good to be there, knowing she was pleased, as she had rehearsed stoically for so many weeks without whimpering complaint.

At the first intermission, Don bought his son and date a cool soda from the solitary concessionaire. Still no disappointment registered on his son's face from their morning defeat. Don was gallant and witty and marked his hurt with sweeping panache. He visited briefly with his wife at the side stagedoor and complimented her profusely on the dramatic first act. She really was good, more animated than he had ever remembered her to be. Strange, he mused, she seems happier now than she does at home. He laughed hollowly to himself. Mistaken must he be, he taunted foxily, no one could be happier than being around him at home. Don burst out laughing, standing alone with his own conversation, and caused a bevy of quizzical faces to swivel curiously in his direction, looking for his non-existent, talkfest Harvey companion.

Don eagerly returned to his seat after the intermission. The air outside had hung wearily, like folds in dusty, heavy theatre curtain. The rich, personally patriotic lyrics of "The Impossible Dream", propelled Don's blood, coursingly hot through his veins. That song, the best known and most enduring selection from the entire production, was a lyrical masterpiece and Don never tired of experiencing the sheer Sousa-like power of the words.

At the conclusion of the performance, the efforts of the repertory company were received as a whopping success. Don beat his hands together until they ached in an effort to applaud for empty seats. The cast garnered unrestrained kudos from the loyal, modest gathering. Almost all the younger set stood at the rear amid vigorous hand smacking. Only a few, dear old ladies stood at the front, those most hearty, but their collective approval there, mustered with allowance for their years, was equally enthusiastic in its own right.

Immediately after the final curtain, Don strolled buoyantly backstage to mix lightly with his wife and the other members of the cast. It was their success and he remained politely on the periphery of their happy contagion, invigorated by their zestful afterglow. They all were buzzing with pride. Contentment emoted from their faces in cracking, smudgy smiles, which emerged trimphantly above pancakes of makeup.

Shading his eyes after the performance, in returning to his parked car, the air outside the theatre, oven hot, stung Don's face when he blinked in the brightness. The return to the cloudless, sultry late afternoon outside thrust him back subconsciously to the bitter disappointment of the morning. Perhaps it was the sharp contrast of glaring brightness and searing heat, when balanced with the dark, cool respite of the theatre that forced Don to relive the match.

He gripped the wheel tightly as he started the ten-mile drive home. He was slipping, slipping. Perilously, he fought to ward off the invasion of depression which macabrely would accompany any mind replay of the match. His brain was screaming. He could not keep the screeching bats of mockery from the cave of his mind. They beat their wings incessantly and flooded his consciousness with black, swarming night as they arrived. The pristine, angelically white, bath of light in his mind that had escaped temporarily from throbbing agony by the deliverance of the magical theatrical performance was rudely dispatched with their hoard-press coming.

Don was a solid tennis player, high club-level in talent, and tennis had been the one opiate in his life around which he had controlled his boozing. Playing good tennis had been important, white-knuckle serious in fact, when his children were infants and Don was winning some local amateur tournaments. His intensity for the game had mellowed somewhat as his children had grown and his interests had changed, but with the arrival of his son, five years earlier, at the threshold of his teen years, Don had focused back to the game with renewed vigor as his son had displayed that innate reservoir of natural talent that needed only to be sprung free in order to gush upward to the height of Don's concluded fulfillment for it.

Hundreds of afternoons, Don and his son had practiced, flailing away at the fuzzy spheroid. Then, their practices had advanced to playful matches, and beyond, to the father-son arena of friendly wars. Early on, Don always won, and his son labored valiantly, measuring his height against the bathroom wall patiently, expectantly, moodily searching for the growth spurt in size and strength that everyone spoke about with decreed certainty.

And then one day, sensing his galloping progress in ability, the son, after one of his razor-close losses, asked his mother if his father would play with him when instead, he started to fashion all the winning scores. She assured him that she thought he would. The breakthrough for the son finally came. Don had felt for months its hot breath, dogging his heel, turning back more and more his racquet artistry. They were having tooth-and-nail, gargantuan battles over that six-month period of play.

Near the medicine chest on a bathroom door at home, Don had posted one of his famous, epistolary signs he was always arranging as gilt-edged dogma for the children, predicting for all, the actual date on which he felt the son would win his first legitimate match against him. His guesswork was uncanny with accuracy. Don missed the momentous occasion by only two days, the son's promised Christmas present for himself that April calendar afternoon when the son burst through finally in victory as a relentless wall of butting sea water crumples a courageous dike of land.

Don had informed his wife unceremoniously, matter-of-factly, that fateful late afternoon, while layering brown, hissing poison over cubes in a tall glass in their kitchen, of the new victory that didn't reside with him. She breathlessly charted his reaction. He offered no alibis. He weathered it well and seemed relieved that the great talent he saw, if it could not be his, was, at least, a part of their own household.

After his fall from dominance, Don continued to play with his son. Occasionally, he would salvage a set, but predictably, the son continued his talent immergence, and Don's future success, more and more, began to wane with each ensuing month. His son's shots zoomed past him like unseeing city buses whisking by waving, puffing commuters, late arriving at bus stops.

Still, he fought on, becoming a battering board for his son's flashing racquet, and loving the experience. His own fantasy, never to be, was there on the court with him, across the net as an integral part of himself.

Don pushed his son because he proclaimed that he needed pushing. His tennis potential was so naturally boundless that Don deemed it essential that he prod and coax him in every possible way. It never occurred to him that its evolution, unfolding as his son would have it unfold, comfortably, naturally, might be a wiser approach in escaping overkill, adolescent burnout, and, thusly, an avoidance later of a toilworn, eventual resentment for the game.

With some reluctance to Don's relentless encouragements, the son, with no teenage place to hide, developed by sheer necessity. He went on to excel in the junior tennis program and Don belched and panted a few years longer in the adult division, through dutiful will and forced commitment, as he couldn't very well stop competing after all the pontificating wisdom about the game he was offering graciously to his son from the benefit of his seemingly infinite experience. Like everything else Don did around the things he loved most, he smothered needlessly, practically to the point of suffocation.

In tennis doubles play, Don was able to endure longer with his son in match-tough competitiveness. His skill and court savvy, now substituted for declining foot speed and reduced mobility, kept their doubles matches interesting and Don was thrilled for that salvation as he was no longer adequate singles competition for his son.

They had played some father-son tournaments and the previous year had earned the ranking of the 5th best father-son team in the state. The matches they lost were a result of Don's lack of physical conditioning. These tournaments were scheduled usually for the summers and Don never played quite as well in the summers. Plagued with excessive perspiration tendencies, Don couldn't keep fluids in his body at that time of year. In the cool fall and winter months, Don's game was sharper.

A year earlier, in a late summer father-son match against stiff state competition, Don nearly had collapsed with heat prostration. Unwisely, he had worn a dark blue shirt on that cloudless, ovenlike day instead of a shirt of reflective white, and again in barely losing at the very end from his lack of stamina, he had been unable to drive away in his car. He had staggered under a tree, mad for shade and coolness, and he had been administered with dousing buckets of ice as he quietly lay there recovering. Twenty minutes later, while judiciously, his son drove them home, Don was slugging down a cold beer.

Don droned along in lazy Sunday afternoon traffic, continuing home from the theatre. Surreptiously, with a silent invasion of havoc-happy vermin, his mind tricked him into a masochistic playback of the morning. This tournament was to have been the last hurrah for Don and his son. Two weeks after it, his son was to leave on scholarship for his freshman year at college in another state, and then, quite predictably, future scheduling of matches together would have been difficult.

Instead of letting the tournament flow normally with success predicated squarely on their racquets, Don had a lot to say before the matches, supposedly psyching his son and himself to frenetic readiness before play even began. They were as good a team as the team that ultimately beat them, perhaps a better team. The sons, both scholarship athletes, were nearly equal in ability, and Don had a great deal more playing experience than the other father.

Don and his son whisked majestically through the early rounds of the competition. The stage became set for the important match that Sunday morning. Their opponents were cocky, loud, and aggressive. That made it worse, they deserved to be beaten. And, at courtside, uncomfortably near, their wife-and-mother camped out, overseeing the whole spectacle.

Don and his son broke ahead early with a 4-2 game lead in the first set. Then it happened, the collapse of the house of cards, the thing Don feared most, unfolded horribly before his very eyes. In the hot summer months, unlike the heart-pacifying cold months, Don could, before his body had its rhythm for the match, sometimes hyperventilate terribly with an early, rapid playing pace, particularly on extremely long points. Then, like an indelicate mixture of pickles and milk, the pressure and tension of the match, when coupled with hyperventilation, became a devastating, unworkable marriage for the physical and mental partners in his body.

His son had seen this situation occur before and had remarked about it openly. Strangely, it only occurred very early in matches, during rapid pace of play, almost as if Don's thermostat had not clicked on yet with the needed voltage. His son knew that once this uncontrolled heavy breathing occurred, Don never really recovered sufficiently to remain tournament-tough in a long match.

And so it happened. This stern crucible of mettle, borne ignominiously on the vulturine wings of doubt, worry, and fear, invaded the match at that point. Don was serving the 4-2 game, the all-important seventh game, the most important game to win in any set so quote the leading authorities on the game. In that game, Don could sense the opposing son begin to flag with concentration as that son had played Don before and knew how well he could play. Fate was cruel however. The game ebbed and flowed, deuce, advantage, deuce, advantage, deuce, advantage and Don, with the intense pressure of wanting to win for himself and his son, was the first one to crack. Don lost the seventh game, the most pivotal of all games in tennis. In winning the seventh game from a 4-2 lead, it takes five straight games by the opposition to wrest a set back their way. But losing the seventh game from a 4-2 lead, means a quick tie once the opposition simply holds their service in the following game.

The tide of battle had been turned. As the match progressed, Don saw his droplets of sweat collect like a generous sprinkling of rain everywhere on the court. Agonizingly, his legs oozed like melting rubber, his movements became awkward, and although his thermostat had clicked on, trying to pace the hyperventilation, the stamina damage that day to his slightly enlarged heart was recorded history.

On long point exchanges, Don tired every time. The match was close all the way, but Don now lacked the clincher. His will was dented by his terrible exhaustion and the haunting memory of the close brush with heat stroke the previous year. Don recounted privately the words of the legendary Vince Lombardi of the Green Bay Packers when he summed it best with his famous epigram---"Fatigue makes cowards of us all."

Don's son was tentative in his play that day because of Don's blustery, bossy approach to his tennis advancement over the years. Don, guided blindly by love and devotion, had always urged and pushed, dragging and extracting the son's great talent from within him. Totally honest in his assessment of his son's unbridled potential he had been, but never had he soft-pedaled the preaching tirades. Through the years, the son had come to play better against his father than with him.

Equality on the court, devoid of natural father and son authoritative pecking order elsewhere, had been Don's watchword. At least he couldn't be faulted for that. The son had capitalized on that freedom of play offered to him and had unburdened his loving upsetness with his father's frustrating ways with expert play against him. The secret, unspoken fear of being blamed unfairly through Don's own fading middle-age ability, transformed the son, quite logically, into a tentative, unsure partner with him.

Don approached his home realizing, for the first time, that in all things now he failed to bring out the best in people. It wasn't just tennis, it was really all endeavors. The match was only a microcosm of a larger unhappiness. His intensity, his approach to things about him, usually resulted in alienation. The comforter blanket of people, earlier sought in life, not needed genuinely now at all he felt, was always heaved aside eventually anyhow, as if discarded by an unseen hand on a fretful, hot stuffy night.

No one stayed close to him for long. Don wasn't an ogre. He didn't stage confrontations or pick at disputes, but, imperceptibly somehow, most people now chose to remain distant from him. This distance is what Don really wanted as he never felt qualified enough to be a real friend in the quicksilver, evanescent definition of the the word. People undoubtedly sensed his design of distance but perhaps incorrectly construed it as aloofness or smugness with them. It really was none of those things, rather, only deep fear and unhappiness with the sad shoddiness of man himself, as an enigmatic creature to behold.

The members of the family arrived home from the theatre in three separate cars at nearly the same time. The daughter had remained home that afternoon, choosing instead, to attend an evening performance later in the following week. It was a festive time, that magical afterglow of a successful theatrical performance for Don's wife. She was chirpy and radiant. Only partially cleaned by a damp washcloth backstage after the performance, her eye makeup riveted slowly down her face in humorous, streaky disarray, comfortably, in the free, homey sense of relaxation. She busied herself in the kitchen with preparation of a roast beef dinner, chortling in the fact that the Sunday matinee had extended a blessed free evening from rehearsals.

Her son came bounding into the house, loosened his tie, and bent to survey a possible pre-dinner pillage of the refrigerator. He heaped his own praise upon the family actress and then surrendered reluctantly to her scolding that a raid of snacks would ruin his appetite for the nice dinner she was preparing for the family.

Don gathered with the family in the kitchen and again offered his effusive, but honest praise with the other critical acclaim bestowed upon his wife. Still, the son showed no remorse from the morning match, and Don continued on stage himself, as the family actor with no real performance of his own in which to star.

Informally, an hour later, the four members of the family assembled at the kitchen table for their roast beef dinner. As they began, expectations were high for a private celebration for the wife. Busy teenage schedules for both children that summer had meant few meals together at one sitting. Everyone laughed about the special occasion now of all four together for dinner.

Don fussed over his roast beef like a petulant, high-chair infant who would not eat. His utensils clattered about his plate. The first dark clouds of the blistering August day formed at the table. Everyone drifted somberly quiet. His teeth, in great need of peridontal surgery, had been bleeding again almost daily. He had delayed care, arguing that he had other places for his money. In order to properly masticate the delicious roast beef, Don would have to suffer for days with sore, bleeding teeth. Embarrassingly, he reluctantly asked that his roast beef be pureed in the blender to facilitate easier chewing. Everyone remained silent and ate politely, not looking up when Don's roast beef pablum returned to the table.

154

The restraint of mood from the match, braced tenuously by adult expectancy only, coupled with the rude reminder of his diseased teeth was too much for Don. He buckled under the strain. His teeth embodied an impossible dream he too had lived that day, isolated off-stage unlike the characters he had witnessed, but somehow on a court-like stage of his own, the monstrous tennis arena of his own creation.

His life rapidly clicked by in frames of kaleidoscopic technicolor. The film was sticking as it unspooled and his aging projector trembled noisily. Quickly and quietly, Don excused himself from the table and somehow stumbled to the privacy of his own bedroom before he cried.

No one in the family ever mentioned that dinner again. Sometimes in the arena of real life, the dragon wins.

TWO TRAGEDIANS

He was born in rural, western North Carolina in the very early part of this century, whittled from the quiet pioneer stock that had peopled those hardy mountains for generations. Families there were typically large, in that beginning era of sputtering motor cars and jerky picture shows, and cooperative effort was required by all from a young age in order to eke out a plain, earthy existence upon the resolute land. Little relaxation or diversion appeared in the paths of chore-bound youths as they cared for each other, expectably, older for younger down the succession, and secondary schooling beyond grade school was an excessive luxury, not a common norm.

When he was eleven, the death of his father hurried him, with necessity, into a premature adulthood. Although he was not the oldest in a family of six children, his plucky resourcefulness and zesty energy soon established him as the unsung, designated leader for the family, a role he would pattern inevitably throughout the whole of his active life.

He grew to medium height, nut-hard, straight and sinewy. Wavy black hair crowned his finely chiseled, wiry body. Prominent cheekbones and a distinctive nose lent a faint hint of his Cherokee Indian heritage, an eighth by blood, from an unchronicled infusion early in the previous century, a scant generation after the American Revolution.

His hands were huge, his fingers long and work-hardened, and his arm-span belied his medium height. His legs were those of a sprinter. In later years he would proudly display his meaty, hairless calves below hastily rolled pant legs and weave folksy yarns of his swift, ball-playing youth.

By trade, he became an iron worker and throughout the halcyon days of the American 1920's and later, during the bitter, soup kitchen days of the following decade, he helped erect famous bridges across San Francisco Bay and other places and he worked on dams in TVA with enduring names like Guntersville, Wheeler, Watts Bar, and Norris. He was always able to find work, even when none seemed available, and he became a beacon for others, a source of jobs for

159

relatives and friends in the dark night of the Depression. His gritty leadership won him foreman status wherever he went and men gravitated to work within the group that he supervised.

His only daughter was born in a tent in northern Alabama in the late 1930's during one of his temporary stays, working there on some emerging iron-and-earth, gargantuan structure. And then, when that edifice gleamed with completion, as an engineering tribute to the ingenuity of man, he packed his family off to another site, following the sun and the hopeful promise of scouted reports of available iron work elsewhere.

Huey P. Long became a casual acquaintance in Baton Rouge when he helped construct the capitol dome there. He often chuckled about the coaxing, fiery spirit of the bayou demagogue, exhorting workers to get on with the job. During World War II, he was part of the secret Oak Ridge project, constructing gray-green, innocuous little buildings which belied the terror which lurked inside them. He took his orders from General Leslie Groves himself, the government watchdog for the genius of J. Robert Oppenheimer. He was a foreman there again with a questioning crew and often he reminisced about the times he fished in the reservoir alongside tight-lipped General Groves, snatching hurried minutes with line and sinker, joyful stolen diversion, from the crunching overtime work race that was demanded from all at this mysterious atomic bomb plant. He told of the clamor at Oak Ridge, the dismay, and the milling, shuffling unsettledness of the workers when they realized that the twin mushroom clouds over Japan in the summer of 1945 indeed had something to do with their work, that vague, indefinite work that was so curious, with every man knowing only a prescribed part of the whole.

After World War II, seeking an end to the nomadic pursuit of work with a sprouting young daughter, he chose plumbing as a trade and opened a shop in a sleepy town in southwest Florida. When the local area spawned a large retirement community, he started a modest furniture store business and

160

with these two business ventures, fashioned a comfortable living.

There he remained for the rest of his working life and also into his retirement years. A fine reputation was enjoyed throughout his life. Everyone called him Lucky, a pleasant sobriquet bestowed on him earlier, as a younger man. His friends in the quiet town, coffee drinking cronies, were judges, county commissioners, doctors, and their friendships were easy, unforced, and reciprocal.

Avidly, he supported his daughter's activities and became quite a favorite among her wide circle of friends. Though his work was rigorous and long, he never appeared too weary to pilot a ski-boat for them in the bay or too tired to show up around a beach cookout fire to narrate some eye-widening, gripping tale.

Almost reverently he immersed himself in the doctrines of one of the world's oldest fraternal orders, and rose among his peers, to claim for a time, the highest local position for that order. Deprived of much formal schooling with his accelerated adulthood, he read omnivorously during the middle part of his life and, self-taught, rounded out an acute awareness on many subjects with a hungry perception that easily would have meant scholar potential had he ever been afforded a real education.

Nimrod, the hunter, and Izaak Walton, the angler, were his unuttered heroes as hunting and fishing were synonymous with his robust appetite for living. When a decision of any kind arose, his favorite retort, accompanied by his twinkling smile, was, "which to do or go fishing." He was happiest calling for wild turkeys on his belly in the nearby Everglades or wading overboard from a boat, rousting oysters with a gloved hand from their stubborn, crusty homes. The end result of his chase with rod and gun always found its way to his bountiful table and often the succulent meals served there by his angelic, stalwart wife were prepared almost totally from the natural pantry of grassy, neighboring fields and from the watery locker of loop-lazy rivers and inland lakes.

As part and parcel of his vigorous outdoor exuberance, a tenderness for nature also prevailed. He understood the beauty and frailty of nature. Patiently, for years, he nurtured orchids in a shade house, experimenting with different strains and varieties, and he reveled in escorting neighbors and friends on botanical safaris into the tropical Everglades, for collecting firsthand those lovely flowers. Many filched, leisure hours, away from his dutiful attendance at work, were spent beneath a pith helmet in his orchid house, coaxing and cajoling plants to glory.

In the evenings, in his living room, slide presentations of beautifully arranged flowers and nature study excursions would entertain. They were striking with their wall-projected brilliance, liquid in dazzling color, against a black velvet backdrop arranged by him for maximum camera effectiveness. His home was bedecked with a profusion of plants and flowers and, on holidays - Easter, Mother's Day, Christmas - he would deliver corsages to the wives of friends. They would be hand delivered, driven around personally, unsolicited gifts from a Good Samaritan florist, freely given for the happiness and appreciation they produced.

He was fiercely and kindly devoted to his daughter. When she chose a potential husband, in that time of early courtship and marriage, the possible son-in-law was tested for his worth, in a nice, polite way, but, nevertheless, he was unquestionably tested. No dragons were unleashed for his lance but he performed other feats for her father. He hacked away for an hour on his knees with a machete to glean the tender, sweet bud of the swamp cabbage. He waded waist deep for twelve hours in Okeechobee Lake, fly-casting for bream with a chest-high Maxwell House coffee can of slittering worms slung around his neck, as his fiancee' fished as well, attired nearby in a devastatingly unreachable bikini.

And once, without warning, on the ruse of needing to move a water-sodden rowboat at his home, Lucky grabbed an end and beckoned the same for the hopeful suitor. The four hundred pound boat was lugged, pantingly, a hundred yards to another spot in the spacious backyard. The only reason for its relocation was to see how the young man would fare and endure. The boat was leaden and covered with slimy algae which thwarted every attempt for a firm grasp. Finally, blind with pain from the clumsy weight, the load was dropped mercifully to the groaning earth. The suitor had weathered the ordeal, which had been sprung craftily upon him. The father, nearly sixty years of age, had carried his half of the small dory without the slightest capitulation or complaint.

During another excursion together, while gathering blackberries near a woodpile, a large snake had slithered into view. The father stalked the elusive serpent through and under the woodpile and thought, in so doing, that he had detected fear on the part of the young man. The fear was slight, only apprehension and disinterest really, but the mild reluctance to be enthusiastic with the rummaging search disturbed him a trifle, such was his paternal love affair with nature and his daughter.

However, the true acceptance of the future son-in-law, the inner circle attainment, came with the eating of fried fish. The father loved fried fish, garnished with hushpuppies and coleslaw. The initiation was complete when the young man was taught to chomp bites off the tails of fried bream. The father was ecstatic. The bream were pan-cooked, after filleting, with their tails intact. He had always bitten off and consumed the tails as a delicacy and when the daughter's suitor displayed no difficulty whatsoever with this atavistic ritual he was back-slapped heartily with family acceptance and the hand of the daughter silver-plattered as a dual reward.

*   *   *

The father, Lucky, was many good things to many people. And, his one glaring inconsistency, his one rude trait, that single, omnipresent, ugly, festering sore in his character, raw and unhealing in its unswerving scope, did not, in and of itself, preclude him from living a good and worthwhile life. Admittedly, it was there, this living yoke, unmistakably real and purposeful in all its tawdry shambles, but judgment passed against it should not condemn alone; rather, only speak as a part of the enigmatic complexity of one man, and as a microcosmic speck of the unfathomed, enigmatic complexity of all men everywhere.

Lucky was a racist, a devout, committed, unadulterated racist. His intolerance and contempt stood out like one chocolate swirl decoration on a white creme pie. The departure of this deep feeling from all the harmony with nature he husbanded, nurtured, glorified, and exalted was remarkably and startlingly incongruous. It was as though the object of his hatred was foreign to nature itself, as if the grand order of things he admired most in the wondrous symmetry of plants, the reoccurring, inspiring marvel of nature touched by the hand of God, did not extend to include Negroes within the purview of those privileged for understanding and love.

When the son-in-law was in his company in the early years of his marriage to his daughter, he would brace and guard himself always for the fusillade of racist venom that dripped inevitably and hideously from the father's mouth. He would appear happy, jovial with the beauty of the day, tender with the luxurious plants swaying to his wand of hand, hospitable and gentlemanly to acquaintances and passersby alike and then, unannounced, a blinding snap would trigger a synapse in his brain and he would launch into a heinous, vitriolic smear of racial hatred. His tar-black eyes would flash, his step would hasten, a clicking sound of resolute authority would emit unconsciously from his clenched teeth and he would flood any listener with a torrent of Caucasian supremacy. The macabre visit from Mr. Hyde would last only moments, never more than a few minutes, and then it would mercifully subside in an instant, and placid Dr. Jekyll would return, until the next time, when the dark stranger came again to pay a shivering visit.

The unpredictable, sudden shifting of personality had a profound effect on the son-in-law. It pushed him farther and farther away from any false illusion with himself. Surely, the son-in-law was grown and had fashioned his own adulthood and, certainly, never had he thought himself tarnished by their association, nor had he envisioned himself as the better man, blessedly without the suffocating choke collar of deep prejudice. No! What it did do, however, was to help drive him farther and farther away from any confrontation with possible duplicity with himself. He chose not to involve himself at all, fearing that the honesty of knowing his limitations made him unworthy for the task before it even began.

The son-in-law knew he was sinful and no great disciple for living himself, but he could understand and accept this circumstance. What he could not understand or accept was how men like the father could live a lifetime wallowing in hate and unbridled prejudice, and hand-in-glove with those elements, as they threaded their way through the riddle of life, elevate themselves to positions of importance in fraternal, church, and civic organizations, and, through it all, never really live within the tenets held up as direction for their very existence, their very purpose, their very reason to be.

The last fifteen words of the creed of his supposed conscience, the creed of one of the world's oldest and most respected orders, reads, "and the guarantee of equal rights to all people everywhere, the end of our contention." Were these only words printed on a page or did they live in truth? Moreover, wondered the son-in-law, had he taken masterfully arranged plants and flowers years before to festoon the clandestine meeting places of the organization blindly followed at that time when he was a younger man, the one frightfully known by those three identical letters, those of the eleventh character in our alphabet?

The father chose, wittingly or unwittingly, to do good in the world, supporting hospitals for children, being a good friend to many men of one color, while living a lie in other areas of his life. The son-in-law came to do very little good in the world, being a friend to few men of any color, while pursuing no lie.

165

Oh! lost! Two men, two puny men, forever lost, forever frail, tossed and scattered leaves in a gale, neither better than the other and both to be pitied and comforted. Two tragedians, unlike and alike, inextricably bound in difference, as one.

The son-in-law tried to accept the father's racism. He wrestled fitfully with his own opinions of it in order to mitigate its rancor. The father had been slung into an adult world early in his youth, made to scratch for himself with the untimely death of his father. He had been deprived schooling and when he found, as a young man, that his innate abilities allowed him to rise to levels of importance in his work, surely he came to resent his roadblocked future through his lack of education. Moreover, his chosen field, heavy construction, meant daily interaction with Negroes, and perhaps he resented his lot and felt that, with a good education, he could have extricated himself from the hard, laborious work in exchange for a vaulting career elsewhere, one more suited to his undeveloped, latent abilities.

Furthermore, it was true, rationalized the son-in-law, as a young man in the late 1920's, the father had sustained a badly broken nose, unguardedly struck by a Negro, while crossing on a makeshift rope bridge at a construction site. He had suffered repeatedly throughout his life with the lingering, nagging effects of that untelegraphed assault.

Few men hate without some reason, albeit unreasonable in its attempt at reasonableness, or without some provocation, some private justification and this knowledge somewhat comforted the son-in-law. Although a proffered peace with Negroes never emanated from the father in his lifetime, the son-in-law, certainly in no august position to pass judgment on anyone, came to accept this dilemma in living as not that of one solitary, misguided man, but one of all men everywhere, stumbling today, walking erect tomorrow, emoting alternatively good and evil, acceptance and rebuke, charitable sharing and hellish covetousness, myopic aloofness and prostrating supplication.

*　　*　　*

"Every man desires to live long but no man would be old," uttered Jonathan Swift. True words indeed! Regretably, the father did not age gracefully. He aged horribly and grew old against his wish. A succession of small, silent strokes, none of which paralyzed him, ravaged him dreadfully, slowly, before the helpless eyes of those who cared for him. Initially, forgetfulness and disorientation would plague him. Sentences and simple thoughts could not be completed. He would sit and shake his head with eyes closed as if to clear his mind for another fresh start with the fuzzy thought but the pauses accomplished little. They lengthened rather, and became the expectation, with only snatches of words coming with any remote meaning or relevance. Apologies became profuse, and he lashed himself sobbingly, and then interminable periods of expressionless silence would follow.

The great columnar strength of his sculptural limbs cracked and chipped, and flew away as invisible dust. A single hand, which once rigged a sectional fly rod deftly, using the natural oil from that area on the cheek near the nose for lubricant between the metal connectors, going alone, expertly, with the other hand quietly paddling a boat, came to fumble an hour with a simple pajama cord or a shirt button. Hands that once filleted fish with the skill and fluidity of a concert pianist and the legerdemain of a tuxedoed magician loosened burning cigarettes to his branded breast. They smoldered their way through cotton cloth unnoticed, until excruciating pain announced their torturing presence.

During his shut-in confinement, the burnished glow of his taut, firm face became gray-yellow, wan and weak, ashen with unruly stubble of jagged beard unevenly kempt, as weeds accumulate randomly at a vacant house. His daughter cared for him with hot dinners whisked to his apartment and constant visits to do his laundry and his housekeeping. During

167

these times, he could be lucid for a flashing moment and recall in infinite detail, a remote happening from years ago. Then, during these unexplained, infrequent glimpses of clear retrospection, he would see also the living horror of his sickness and he would comment pitifully on his condition as if he knew full well what was happening to him. Then, mercifully, he would be allowed to lapse again into a stupefied state with his loss of dignity no longer mirrored back to torment him.

As his condition progressively worsened, accommodations for his perpetual care were readied for him at the home of the daughter and son-in-law. He was moved early, before the renovations were completed, when he was discovered sitting one day at his apartment, unable to explain himself, with a quizzical, poking finger gesturing toward all four, coiled burners of his stove, orange hot for use, lit for hours, for no cooking reason.

His stay with his daughter and her family, a labor for her of true love devoid of any real reason, torn from the heart alone, was short-lived, and doomed from its inception. His living death was accelerating out of control. Scolded and admonished like a child, for his own safety, he seemed to understand but then, moments later, he would babble incoherently and injure himself in venturing off, rambling up and down forbidden stairs, stumbling and falling to the floor. He was unmanageable.

Every member of the household had an assignment for his care but the plan floundered miserably, to no avail and without success. The daughter and son-in-law had careers outside the home and their children attended school. His strayings from safety couldn't be controlled and he couldn't be restrained from hurting himself. In a few short weeks, he was moved again to a nursing home where professional care and constant monitoring were provided. Sadness for some, relief sprinkled with sadness for others, the decision was the only logical alternative. There was simply no other choice.

The son-in-law had persevered at home as best he was able with the horror of the father's innocent, naked wanderings, balancing his way along halls, supported by walls, while trailing excrement uncontrollably with every halting, howling step. It was he, the son-in-law, who deemed his maintenance impossible, his home care burdensome beyond sanity. In the final analysis, he was probably right. But, admittedly the son-in-law never did well with break from known, comfortable routine or with deeds of great compassion beyond the implementation of flowery rhetoric.

The last days for the father were not pleasant. His nocturnal escapades about the ward, only a few feet from his bed, invariably ended with collapse to the floor and injuries always resulted. The dead of night phone calls came and came. Then, restraints, seemingly cruel but necessary, were applied to his bed, but still, to the utter amazement of orderlies and nurses, he managed to slip free occasionally, only to crumple immediately to an unforgiving tile floor.

The fall of a once proud, indomitable man to the relegation of a drooling, dependant incompetent was so dramatically and so vividly pronounced that its stark fear would have transformed the most confirmed, swaggering atheist into a kneeling, quaking, cringing, reformed beggar of God's forgiveness and acceptance.

No one knew if he suffered with pain near the end. Hopefully, he did not. The wild terror in his eyes, marvelously calmed in repose of ensuing death, urged a desperate plea for a swift passing as if he knew how he must look to others and how he hated his inexorable plight and their hopeless, vigilant burden.

At the end, no conversation murmured, no physical vestige of youth remained, no joy of understanding expiated, and he endured those last unspeaking, chilling days unable to argue, debate, defend or reconcile any of the enigmatic ways of the world, with even his closely reclined ward mate, a man as sick as he, the old gentleman in the adjoining bed, the only member of that race in the entire nursing home, the Negro lying and dying beside him.

169

THE BLADE

Denim clad and sporting a one day shadow of Saturday stubble, Harry, swearing aloud to no one, hoisted his lawn mower up to the rear hatchback door and grumbling further, still to no one, pantingly shoved and slid the clumsy machine well forward up into the flat bed of his station wagon so he could close the door behind it.

Harry was put out with himself. Again the blade of this mower wouldn't cut butter forgotten on a summer picnic table. Another Saturday morning ruined, he thought to himself. He had wanted to trim his lawn and finish all of his self-assigned little gardening chores so he could collapse later, guiltlessly, before his television shrine at home when the panorama of sports viewing began that afternoon. But now, the valuable start he had engineered in crashing about his yard before most people had even stirred to wakefulness, was lost. The damning trip to the mower repair shop would consume half the morning even if he were lucky enough not to have to leave the blasted thing.

Still muttering to himself, Harry, with eyes darting left then right, flew out of his driveway, rattling the mower riding behind him. He could hear the gurgle wash of gasoline in the little tank and slowed appreciably. Three times he calculated as he drove, three times in just over a year that lousy blade needed sharpening. Where the hell was that blade forged anyhow, questioned Harry unspokenly. Outer Mongolia? Harry laughed to himself, self-indulgently, stingily, amid his proclaimed torture of misery. He confessed that he was pleased with his one-liner on non-existent steel mills in the Gobi Desert.

Soon, however, he was again scowling. With the arching sun now leading its boiling march overhead, Harry, still knotted in frustration, could only view the day as fleeting, with himself at its epicenter, inert and powerless in its grasp, thwartly unable to complete the design he had planned for it. He chose not to pivot mentally, positively, from the disappointment with his dull blade, chose not to savor the day in its undemanding presence, chose not to pluck its proffered

173

fruit of freedom as a time gift for some interesting pursuit or adventure. Rather, he chose to disrupt the fineness of the new day with peevish, fretful unhappiness over his sudden problem of having yet another dull mower blade.

Despite the early hour, the mower repair shop with the hardware store in the front, or the hardware store with the mower repair shop in the rear, depending upon your point of view and the immediacy of your need, was alive with scurrying Saturday patrons. Fortunately for Harry, the throng of customers had gathered chiefly toward the front, selecting the hardware items of the season - sprinklers, garden hoses, seed, and fertilizer.

Only one person at the mower repair area had preceded Harry there with a problem. Harry squirmed foolishly over his dumb luck of being second, failing to realize that he would have been twentieth in the line at the hardware cash registers nearby. And, even with that eventuality, only a modest annoyance would have been classified normal or arguably allowable by any "prudent man" standard. Yet, Harry fretted.

Delicately, saving his lower back, Harry clattered his mower to the ground and, without benefit of engine, wheeled it manually up the inclined ramp and jaringly parked it abruptly, close to the only other mower before him in line.

The repairman, Wesley, a chunky, pleasantly unassuming man in his early sixties, with whom Harry had conducted lawnmower business on at least a dozen occasions during the past decade, and the other customer peered questioningly at the kiss-near stoppage of Harry's mower, and then their gaze, pleadingly, without verbal complaint, swung up and engaged Harry's eyes. Harry backed his mower away by two feet and clopped heavy-footedly away from them, pacing toward and hastily inspecting, without any real interest, the neat, drawn together, red-tagged repaired mowers, columned in nearby rows, silently awaiting the return of their masters.

During those edgy moments before he was able to speak to Wesley, his possible Saturday morning savior for continued chore activity, Harry wrestled with the right entreaty to use in order to persuade Wesley to sharpen the blade now, while he waited.

The last thing he wanted to happen was to have to check in the mower and leave it. Damn it, Harry determined, if he could get him to sharpen that blade now he could rush back home and still finish what he had begun that morning by the time the singing of the national anthem signaled the start of the game that afternoon. He knew Wesley, casually, with lawn mowers being their only common bond. Now, he wished he had spent more time over the years dutifully capturing Wesley's friendship.

When Wesley was ready for his new patient, Harry's mower, a crying towel approach had been selected for his opening gambit.

"Of all the dumb luck," Harry blurted, furrowing his forehead and squinching his eyes dramatically, "Had a good head of steam going and found this blade so dull again I could do a better job with scissors. Wow! Would I ever appreciate you sharpening that blade now. Got all kinds of plans later and I can still finish them if you can do it now. I mean, uh, wouldn't it be great? There's a chance you can right? Come on, say yes!"

It wasn't November in any election year, but had it been, Harry would have been a viable, legitimate hopeful in any political race, so Oscaresque was his acting performance.

"Always a chance," replied Wesley, noncommittally, with a lifetime of ponderous experience in diagnosing cancerous mowers, terminal beyond repair and others which were only a little sick, perhaps with a treatable engine virus.

"Let's have a look," Wesley continued vapidly. He weighed the handle down with a concrete block, ever present on his workbench for that purpose and, with the mower skirting tilted luridly in the air, he examined the underparts. He probed and poked like a physician, making sure the blade housing was stable and secure. With assurance of that fact, he lightly skimmed an oily, work-chipped hand over the cutting edge of the blade.

175

"Dull as a B Cowboy movie," deadpanned Wesley. Harry seized his encouragement drum again and beat it resoundingly.

"Can be fixed easily, right? No big job, right?" he entreated with inflection in his voice that practically removed all possible rebuttal.

Wesley filled air in his mouth, inflating his cheeks to fullness and then slowly released the pressure, with the escaping hiss of a punctured tire, and remained silent, debatingly, assessing his mental timeclock. He sorted either placation for Harry in sharpening the blade now or, instead, the logging in of the machine for attention sometime later in the following week.

"Not too busy this morning. Strange. Have been on Saturday all summer," granted Wesley dispassionately.

"Then...then, you'll do it, right? Now, I mean. Super deal," summarized Harry, seemingly blocking all retreat. Harry patted Wesley's perspiring shoulder gratefully and then dried his clammy hand secretly across the seat of his own jeans.

Wesley surveyed the exterior of the mower, carded globs of wet sand from the nicked orange metal, gauged the oil dipstick, and blew at the carburetor with his eyes tightly closed. Harry shifted his hands nervously from his hips to his belt loops, stuffed them down his rear pockets and then to a folded cradle across his chest. Having completed these movements, he ran through the entire routine again in the same fidgety sequence.

Wesley spoke next, measuring his words carefully and distinctively. "I'm sorry you're so unhappy."

Harry pounced on the change of topic like a salesman offering a pen to a customer in a check writing mood, now interpreting Wesley's remark as certainly no refusal to his blade sharpening plea.

"Shucks, who wouldn't be unhappy. Back that hunk of metal out of the shed only to find it tangle over a one week growth of summer grass. Hell! Unhappy, yes. But you are making it a lot easier, sharpening the blade now." Harry held his breath, frozenly hopeful that his soliloquy had been persuasive enough.

"That's not what I meant," Wesley replied quietly. Then haltingly, he added, "I meant I'm sorry you're unhappy generally."

Harry was taken back a step. "What, uh, what was that? Say again!" puzzled Harry. He bumped into a packing case and then leaned back against it for support. "Repeat that, would you? Am I hearing right?" questioned Harry with incredulity.

"Don't get sore. I didn't mean any offense. Just sorry you're so unhappy," defended Wesley.

With the blade now detached from the mower, Wesley had started the blade sharpening process, so Harry reversed his sugary tactics in the face of Wesley's startling statement and angrily demanded an explanation, deducing Wesley could not very well fail to finish sharpening the blade now that he had begun. Harry looked bewilderingly about the little shop and found no one within earshot so he leveled both barrels and fired.

"Will there be any charge for my Saturday morning office visit, Sigmund? Jesus Christ, I mean I do appreciate you sharpening the blade but will there by any charge for the counseling too?"

"No charge and I meant no harm," Wesley reassured apologetically.

"No, it's okay, have at it," continued Harry sarcastically. "I wasn't doing anything anyhow this morning. Slap my face! I mean the day started out bad, so I guess anybody can take a potshot at me." Harry clapped his open palms against his outer thighs and awaited a response from Wesley. It came after an eternal pause, as obscure as Wesley's opening remark.

"You were doing something. You were trying to do something this morning. You were trying to mow sand again."

Harry braced himself with one hand on the packing case and roughly ruled his hair with the other. Nonplussed, he fretted, then stormily, he lashed out at Wesley. "Mowing sand! Mowing sand! Listen, you mind if I call you 'ole timer' and not Sigmund? I mean we've scarcely said hello in the past and now this morning you are laying some heavy words on me, and, well, 'ole timer' just seems to fit you. I mean, I can give you a nickname, right? Fair's fair! Nothing personal. I mean, first, you say I'm unhappy and now you say I mow sand. What's next?"

"Nothing next. 'Ole timer' is fine, no offense," permitted Wesley.

"Great! I feel better," Harry answered condescendingly.

Wesley filed the blade manually with sweeping strokes from a rough-notched rasp. Then he whirred the blade over an electric wirebursh. Harry squirmed, wanting to speak, but he couldn't speak and be heard above the piercing spurts of blade-sharpening noise. Harry hunched and sagged his shoulders repeatedly, anxious for the silent pauses interspersed between Wesley's ear-shattering work maneuvers, so that he could interrupt with a flood of questions.

"Carry on 'ole timer', tell me more, this is getting interesting," continued Harry bravely, self-assured that no corpus delecti would be located in his case and that he would be exonerated conclusively from any accusation Wesley had suggested.

"You really want me to go on?" replied Wesley sparingly.

"Well, hell yes. I mean there's no extra charge for the wisdom, right? I'm unhappy and I mow sand you said. Speak on, learned sage. Sherlock Holmes theatre right here in your friendly neighborhood mower shop. What...what, uh what clues have you got?"

Harry stumbled over those words, just noticeably, with his voice a little shaky and somewhat higher in pitch. Any lie detector test would have proved interesting at that moment. This soliloquy did not rank with his earlier Hamlet and MacBeth triumphs when he cajoled Wesley into sharpening the blade while he waited.

"Partly this, partly that," returned Wesley, again measuring his words politely, without noticeable rancor.

"Meaning?" coached Harry, with a faint, greenish clamminess now fighting his purpled neck for territorial rights.

178

As he labored on at his workbench, Wesley, without fanfare, set forth his unwritten brief for Harry's day in Wesley's court. His canvas work apron, held about his ample waist by a rawhide cord, his well-greased and time-tattered, name-stitched workshirt, and his plastic goggles perched against his forehead like a grotesque second pair of reptilian eyes, belied any mistaken identities for professional credits in either the field of psychology or criminology. Yet, those credentials could have been his too, in addition to his hard-knock doctorate in mower repairing.

"Maybe have fifty customers out where you live. Know the streets. Indian and animal names. Fellas been bringin' mowers in for years from out there."

"You're the closest shop around to us," fanned Harry with burning curiosity.

"Know what grows out there and what don't," pursued Wesley, jerking a thumb toward the hardware section up front where fertilizer sales had chimed the cash registers there for years.

"Oak trees everywhere competin' for soil nutrients and sunlight. Hard for grass to grow, 'specially on your street on the creek, where oak trees the heavies'!"

Harry felt queasy. He shifted his feet nervously like a captured truant before a stern principal, but he remained silent, eager for Wesley to continue.

"So, guys like you, after a while, end up mowing sand, without realizin' it. Plain 'nough. Nothin' dulls a mower blade as quick as sand. Weeds don't. Nothin'"

Harry was speechless. Hurt and relief combined in a unsettling concoction of reaction. He realized that the 'ole timer' had struck a nerve, a nerve he had not felt twinge before, a nerve that had lain hidden and dormant, unseen, untouched, or simply unassailed by friend and acquaintance alike.

Intrigued, Harry boldly cast out more bait, flicking it with his tongue, like the hopeful light plopping of a fishing lure to a shady, beckoning spot. "What...what, does..., well..., mowing

179

sand...if...if sand, mind you, is...uh...mowed, I mean, have to do with, uh!... say unhappiness?" Harry's back was icily damp against his clinging denim workshirt and he slumped back against the wooden packing case again.

Wesley ground the blade again at his lathe with the accompanying shrill whirring again precluding conversation and Harry agonized impatiently. Then Wesley casually pawed for a wrench in a cluttered drawer, unconsciously abetting the drama of the moment.

"Well, you complete the picture yourself. It don't take no genius."

"Me?" queried Harry, not understanding.

"Sure, you."

Still Wesley hunted for the right wrench. He rummaged through another drawer. Then, after a glacial epoch in gnawing anticipation he resumed, "You got a well kept car, you dress neat, you're in good shape for your age, so it ain't no mystery you care 'bout yourself and stuff. Chances are, as I see it, you are just actin' out some stubborn stick-to-it kind of thing from being taught as a kid, without realizing it. You ain't a quitter and there's your sand mowing."

Harry, ashen-faced with shock, was totally supported by the packing case. Tottering against it, he glanced about him for a chair, found a folding one, and meekly dragged it near to Wesley's bench and heaved himself into it, straddling it backwards. The body language was unmistakable. The peacepipe had been offered. The fight and agitation were gone, no longer was Harry defensive. He was vulnerable now, pliant for molding, startled, yet relieved by the mental purgation offered to him.

"Amazing," Harry murmured awkwardly.

"You're successful, but somethin' got you on a treadmill. Can't get off. You just mow sand, numb like, 'cause a man in the nice suburbs should keep his place up. You're tough. You don't know what to do, so you mow on."

A home movie clicked mockingly through Harry's mind. Wesley, his 'ole timer', the sagacious mower repair man, had

180

exposed his flank and Harry knew it. Yes, he was now mowing more sand than grass. The cluster of oak trees at home, over a hundred saplings he had numbered ten years earlier when they were young, had proliferated, blocking the sun with their stretching canopy of branches. Hungrily these trees had competed with the grass for nutrients in the soil and, uncompromisingly, with their sun-devouring appetite, the trees had stunted the life pursuit of the grass. Their brown leaves in autumn had lightly sprinkled the ground in their plummet as young trees. With mature growth their leaves now fell in brown blizzards, smothering the grass each year in ankle-deep carpets of suffocation. The big, brawny trees with their insatiable quest for sun and nourishment had wasted the grass. The grass had lost.

Painstakingly, Harry, through the years, had patched the sandy earth beneath the leaves with sprigs of new grass but his efforts had proved ever futile. The lordly trees ruled the yard domain of his home. Every autumn, he, his son, and others battled the leaves with weeks of raking siege. However, this enemy was never contained, the struggle was never won, only lost painfully, imperceptibly, by slipping degrees, each year.

One Saturday morning in the early winter past, both Harry and his son had rested their chins dejectedly on their rake handles, bone weary from their war against the pitiless drift of dead, dry leaves, and his son had remarked, "Dad, the leaves just lying there look better than the bare ground."

Harry had agreed reluctantly and moments later they had returned their rakes to the little shed, as the vanquished stack their rifles before a conquering general, and they had trudged slowly back up to the house from the creek bank.

"Where did you go?" Wesley asked, verbally shaking Harry from his flashback trance.

"What...What?" stammered Harry.

"Where did you go?" repeated Wesley. "I was talking to you. You were listening, then you weren't."

"Oh, I...I...I guess I was thinking. Sorry. Say, the ...uh... other guys, I mean those out my way who came in, are they, some that is, unhappy? I...I mean, who you say are unhappy?"

Wesley stroked his gray, stubbled chin and altered his goggles slightly so that his red-pinched forehead would experience two different blood-depleted circles. "Hm'm, four or five, I'd say," mused Wesley, "Mebbe six."

"And...and what are they like? I...I mean I wouldn't want any names or anything like that."

"Wouldn't give no names, natch'ly," reassured Wesley. "Oh! they're like you. Good guys with carin', just gettin' eat up with unhappiness that is gonna ruin 'em if they don't wake up."

"Did you...uh...do you, I mean did you ever tell them, like you told me?"

Harry needlessly inched his chair closer to Wesley's workbench for privacy but no one had sauntered back from hardware and no new mower customer had arrived. They remained alone. Wesley had finished sharpening the blade and was fitting the gleaming result back on the underhousing of the mower.

"I did."

"And?" Harry ventured breathlessly.

"They got mad at first. Huffy. Wouldn't come back at first."

"Then?"

"Got to know all of them by name later. Two of them even bring a thermos of coffee 'bout once a month, real early on a Saturday and we pitch pennies and play a little penny-ante. Nothin' big mind you. Comin' next Saturday in fact. 'magine, one a medical doctor and the other, a fancy big company 'xecutive, visitin' with a broke-down old mower repairman like me."

"Amazing," said Harry.

"Yeah, ain't it. Hard to figure."

Now it was Harry's turn to be lucid with wisdom and he seized the opportunity. "That's not really what I meant," smirked Harry. "Sound familiar?"

"Don't follow?" questioned Wesley.

"Like you setting me straight a few minutes ago."

"Oh! Yeah, that." Wesley's fine mind, uneducated but streetwise, comprehended and he laughed. He waited for Harry to make his point.

"You told them the truth, something they long suspected but no phony around them ever had the guts to say. You were no threat to them. They knew that. You spoke from the heart. To put it bluntly, you gave them a mind enema. All people need that but what is so tragic out there in that jungle where I operate, is that few people even know how to ask for help. Pride. Foolish pride. Killed many a good man. Oh Christ! Listen to me would you. You're the analyst 'ole timer', not me. I'll shut up. Tell me what to do about the grass."

Wesley lowered the mower to the ground and cranked the engine to test the carburetor adjustment he had made. It trembled to life with his first pull of the cord.

"Well, I'd say the healthy minds out your way recognize it for what it is. I mean the ones who roll with the punches kinda like. Soil poor. Trees a plenty. Trees will win. They plant ferns, put in rock, let the leaves lay. Ever try enjoyin' the trees for just them? I'd say they just sorta make their own peace with the mower blade, so to speak. Mebbe that's what you need to do. Find the problem, the unhappiness, the thing that makes you mow sand. Wife? Kids?" tested Wesley timidly.

"No, not them," disallowed Harry, wagging an index finger while shaking a disclaimer with his head. "Career...career. Always the career. Can't control my own destiny. Job won't allow it. So stumble tired over my career all the time that when nature, your trees I mean, just kept coming, it kind of beat me down. A double vise like."

He pushed his palms together as bookends. Wesley nodded ruefully. Then Harry slowly rose, sighed deeply, and slid the folding chair back to the spot from which he had borrowed it. He paid Wesley in cash with green bills peeled off a money clip which had been hidden securely in his jeans pockets.

He guided the repaired mower back down the ramp, outside to his car. Wesley followed him and together they hoisted the mower with the rejuvenated blade up into the rear of the station wagon. Wesley returned up the ramp and stood there, framed in the open doorway, facing down at Harry, with one work-creased, greasy hand held above him against the door jamb.

"Well," experimented Wesley, earnestly, too frank for sarcasm, "will I ever see you again, I mean, now that I shot my mouth off?"

Harry salivated over the vulnerable opening Wesley had provided for a great one-liner retort. He recounted the one about the Gobi Desert and no steel mills that he had fashioned privately for himself on the drive over an hour earlier. Wesley's candor had stripped him to nakedness with himself. His agitation was gone, he could laugh now. Mischievous elves frolicked across Harry's mind and his lips twitched excitedly.

"Maybe not," he replied thoughtfully after a long pause. He parceled out his answer tantalizingly, with the perfect timing of a standup comedian. Wesley's face slumped with displeasure. "I may do something about my blade instead." Harry had savored the moment diabolically but he couldn't come to prolong Wesley's suspenseful disappointment.

Wesley understood. His smudged face erupted with satisfaction, revealing crooked teeth in varying stages of aging disrepair. An unchecked smile cascaded to his fuzzy chin.

"No, ole timer. The truth can hurt, but, by God, it's better than the alternative, as the saying goes. Foolish pride won't trap me. Besides, I'm tough, right? You told me so. I mow sand, remember?"

Harry opened his driver door and readied his departure, making sure with a final glance that the mower was secure for the ride home. He slid behind the wheel and propped his forearm out the open window.

"Say, I was wondering, not to horn in mind you, but if it would be okay, just on kind of a trial basis really, uh, could I bring my own thermos of coffee next Saturday and come down? I've never pitched pennies with a doctor and a big

184

company executive. Could I drop by?"

Wesley nodded approval immediately and continued to smile broadly.

ON THE TRAIL

My excitement mounts about me like hot, steaming water edging up in a weary traveler's bathtub. It wells with soothing gurgle, rising, deepening, rippling lightly as it builds, intensifying in its vaporific warmth and in its singing maiden promise of sweet satisfaction and I am delirious with its beckoning expectation, as I am on the trail.

My excitement brims as I submerge myself slowly, gingerly, sighingly, with toe sensor tingle into the mind bath I have drawn for myself. My body, now as a gently rocking boat on calming waters, settles down, eases down, slaps itself playfully against the limpid ripples, and I am awash in a drugless, psychedelic state of euphoria, as I am on the trail.

My whole being is idling now, purring now, finely tuned now, my tiny blue pill, hypertensive crutch for survival is heaved aside evangelically and clatters away from me. I walk on alone, as in the New Testament lesson, exultant, reborn, without support, without my crutch.

My jangling, puppet-strung, dishrag-wrung mind, fettered at home to Alexander's black box icon, is unleashed for an exploring, sniffing, lung expanding run, as a hunting dog darts, noses, bounds and barks excitedly, once released from his cage of confinement.

And I am ecstatic, as Alexander's octopal cord cannot reach me, cannot entwine me, cannot strangle me, and I will not be blamed, harrassed, scolded, made to apologize without fault, for I cannot be found. Only God sees my speck there, my insignificance there, and prayfully He does not disclose my refuge, my seclusion, my meditation on the trail.

At Dick's Gap, in northeastern Georgia, one of the several hundred entry points along the 1,995 mile Appalachian Trail, which extends from Maine to Georgia, we leave Granny safely locked away in the car. Shawled and capped, she reads contentedly, propped aslant against her driver door, to seek the reluctant, oblique sun of late October, which filters through her window from the south.

The other three of us, generations of matching surname and gender, unfold exuberantly from the car, invigorated by the cool autumn air. We wave goodbye and leave her for a few hours. She doesn't mind. She is safe, near the highway, parked at the wayside overlook. She will read and nap, then nap and read.

We traipse up over picnic benches, and dodge through stands of permanent outdoor grills and anchored refuse cans. And then, magically, we disappear, transformed by the brutish yet tender snare of the trail. We struggle not in its grasp. We surrender willfully, strung out single file, vulnerably exposed within its hallowed lair, at its regal mercy.

Cut saplings, arranged by caring environmentalists, mark the border entrance as we enter. We go up steeply and make an abrupt left turn to higher ground. Vegetation, a blend of fall russet and summer green, closes behind us. We are imprisoned happily like a hungry street bum in a cozy jail at chilling Christmas time.

The trail is rough with rocks. Our progress requires measured, deliberate step. The way is clear, somewhat easily found and followed, but strewn among the rocks are twigs and branches which, while orchestrating further the natural allure of the trail, render passage slippery and tedious. We are careful not to turn an ankle.

Grandad, senior surname, pants and stops. He goes on ahead, leading, then pants and stops again. He grinds his walking stick in the earth and craftily supports himself against it. We notice. He apologizes profusely about his panting, unable to disguise it from us. We make no fun of him. We understand. All grandads pant on mountain trails. We will be grandads too one day, and then we will pant. He need not apologize.

Middle surname pants a little too. He pants openly in the company of senior surname but turns and tries to hide his panting from young surname, judging it expedient to disguise, for now, his clay-footed shortness of breath from him. Young surname pants not at all. He is sleek and fit and would not pant if he ran backwards up the trail.

Ah! The innocence of youth. On second thought, consider

wisdom. Perhaps they are not as innocent as they are wise. We, who are older, could be wise with our panting, open with it, as innocent as youth, but we are not. Only with our age do we lose our innocence and disguise our panting. Young surname is wise to our ways and says nothing. He understands.

As we ascend, we pause periodically to sling rocks down the broad ravine to our right. The woods are still, so still, save for our whistling rocks, which thunderously startle the silence. The rocks are brown, heavy and smooth and they do not crumple easily as Florida limestone and coquina rocks disintegrate at home. We skip them down the embankment and grade the toss of each other. Some career lightly off objects and reverberate well down the ravine; others, end their flight abruptly, clunking into trees and stumps. Grandad always has the best toss. We see to that. We compliment him. He smiles broadly.

We reach the top, our top, at the old, dead tree. The trail goes on, to the state of Maine, skirting farmland and factory alike, if we choose to continue but we stop here. Grandad leads us off fifty yards to the west and shows us again the old campfire cairn of stones, and then, in scoutmaster fashion, he challenges us to find the old, dead tree again. We hesitate for effect and then routinely point it out through the tangle of undergrowth. He noddingly approves our merit badges, won fairly in the wild, on the trail. He leads us back to the old, dead tree. Following him, middle and young surname wink at each other. No one is wiser and no one is hurt.

Grandad explores about the old, dead tree, searching in radiating circles for blue and white direction markings, emblazoned on trees. He pulls from his jacket pocket again this year the worn, creased pamphlet that describes the meaning of the markings. He explains their differences to us again. He recites the sixteen points of the compass to all who would listen, and then quotes all his German phrases to invisible chipmunks and squirrels. He points beyond our station to where he ventured on alone one year, well past our dead tree landmark. He pops a beer, one of several that have been lugged patiently up the incline, stowed within his heavy jacket, blessedly reserved for consumption now, with reflection, reminiscence, and "medicinal purpose" ardor. Then he wanders off privately to commune with a call from nature.

Middle and young surname sit together on a log during Grandad's brief absence. Young surname suffers through all the questions put to him about college tennis and college studies. Middle surname seldom relaxes with him and always talks about these topics. Never does he vary the interrogation but he can't help himself. Middle surname knows his failing but he can't change, wishing so for young surname to achieve so much more than he ever accomplished. Young surname understands all, answers all, achieves all.

Unexpectedly, Grandad returns and shouts, "This is the life of Riley," to the surrounding sentinels of pine and oak. His throaty exhilaration bounces off hill and dale like a darting, silver pinball lighting up lights in collision, and then it echoes away, lost about us, and again all is still.

Grandad addresses young surname affectionately as "ole fella" and pokes playfully at him with his walking stick. Then he belches indecorously from his gaseous beer and apologizes to the whole forest with his inimitable, "explain everything" favorite French trademark - "Sacre Bleue."

With a sigh of age, Grandad stagily folds down to join us on the log. We stir our numb rumps with restless shifting upon the unforgiving seat and then settle back down for our brief, perennial scientific lecture on the merits of alcohol over water.

Grandad pops another beer as ready exhibit for his lecture. He explains unswervingly that water rusts pipes and inquires disarmingly if we agree. He is so convincing with his soiled soliloquy. We meekly acquiesce, fighting back rollicking laughter. Then Grandad holds his beer aloft as one would gloat with a rare, dusty treasure unearthed from antiquity and explains that alcohol doesn't rust pipes or a single esophagus, but rather is used widely as a disinfectant and as a cleaning agent. Therefore, he concludes, wanting to be clean, which he

192

conveniently marries up with health, he drinks beer instead of water. We restrain ourselves, knocking our knees to each other for support in stoical silence. Grandad capitulates first, with a fount of laughter. Riotously, we join him in unbridled laughter of our own. We all understand this time.

Grandad hushes us quiet and we listen to the woods for a time. Far below us, near Granny, a truck groans and labors on the curving, elevating mountain road. Middle surname bristles, fearing it is omnipresent Alexander and his black box creation coming to fetch him back to civilization. He collects himself and repels the thought only to spot through the canopy of trees, a giant jetliner, an insect speck above, barely visible with its great height. Instinctively, middle surname ducks under a spray of leaves, hopeful not to be sighted from the air.

We descend. No panting emits now from anyone. We are at ease now with gravity in our camp, as our abiding ally. Rocks and pebbles scurry downward, dislodged by our skidding feet. We dawdle, we mope, devouring our love with the trail, knowing a rapid descent means bittersweet separation from our loved one.

We approach a fork in the trail. Middle surname suggests a new way down, to the right. Miraculously, Grandad, always comfortable with the known routine to the left, agrees to a new adventure down on the strange route. The path bends to the right, then left again, winds lower, and all are eager with the new experience. Grandad points out tree blazes on our discovery fork and announces reluctantly that we are not the original pathfinders.

Bursting through to a clearing, we see the paved road and close by, our car with Granny still safe inside. We cluster together on folding chairs at the end of our return. Grandad surveys his domain with lordly pride. A piece of old tennis towel from years gone by wraps around his perspiring neck. He has another beer and waves to passing motorists, and they are friendly with return greetings.

Granny negotiates our leave for the trip back to our mountain lodge with an eternal turning of the car on the shoulder of the road. Although he is able to do so, Grandad won't drive back, as he has protected his pipes from rust all afternoon. He knits his lips, and wags his head for a vacant view out his window while Granny wrestles the steering wheel.

Granny is a good driver, slow and steady, with two hands on the wheel at all times. Cars, like nudging dominoes collect behind us on the serpentine, double-lined mountain road. Then, on the short, straight passing chances they zoom past with an edgy honk of horn or with a lolling, rolling head of impatience. She doesn't mind. She is a good driver.

We plan the morrow together. Where will we go in our beloved mountains? Those two in the back seat lovingly pat those in the front seat. Grandad swivels his head to those behind him and pokes a finger toward them. Granny's eyes never leave the road but she smiles. Country-style visions of buttered grits, tangy sausage, red-eye gravy, smoking biscuits, dance like sugarplums fairies in our heads. We exalt these breakfasts, renowned at our mountain lodge, where we stay each year.

Jokingly, we reflect on the evening ahead in our trusty room 113, conjuring up fantastic plans of blaring stereo music, picture puzzles forming on card tables, late television comedy piercing our darkened room, backgammon and pinochle games progressing in every corner. We boast of square-dancing and clogging until dawn down in the village near our lodge.

We are happy with fatigue and activities discussed for evening exist each year only in our fertile imaginations. At seven o'clock we are in the lap of the mountains, early to bed, and asleep, as nothing further can ever top the day we have had. On the morrow we will do again what we always do, hike on the trail, but it becomes never commonplace, never stale, never satiable, for our rapture, our joy, our oneness is as steadfast and as timeless as the trail itself.

A TIME OF GOODBYE

A brace of cool, green trees, fed by a ribbon of winding creek, bordered the field to the west. At right angles to these trees, and meeting the creek at its end, a quiet, dusty road, seldom traveled, ran the length of the field on the north. The road ended abruptly now at the creek. The bridge there, built in horse-and-wagon days, was dilapidated beyond repair, with only a few splintered, creosoted pilings standing to mark its proud usage, over a half century ago.

Across the broad expanse of the rectangular field, nearly a mile to the east, two modest ranches, neat and unpretentious, with one boosting a windmill skyward above a deep water well, formed a pioneer stock permanence to that border of the field.

However, these buffers of protection on three sides for the field regrettably did not extend to the fourth side, its southern extremity. On that side, the vulnerable underbelly of the field lay unprotected, as gates to a frontier fort carelessly swung open and forgotten. Rudely exposed there the bucolic charm of the field was interrupted by an ever closing, relentless parade of development homes. There, the present agony for the field had begun. Its dismal future and inevitable demise had been charted, mapped, and schemed, and now its final dirge, hastily and poorly composed, was being stridently performed.

A neighbor to the field had come to visit there often. On Sundays, as on this very day, he would come for long, restful walks. Through the years, he had been there also in the early weekday evenings; in winter, at the moment of slanting fire-red sunset, and in summer, during the wet, sticky, lingering hours of summer nightfall.

Beyond the dusty road to the north of the field, hidden by a choke of wooded thickets, a sprawling, upper middle class neighborhood thrived. It backed up to the field, separated from it by the trees and the dusty, lonely road but it did not front on the field at all. Curiously, few people from the throng of those who lived there knew of the field and even fewer ever visited or even once gazed across it.

197

But their neighbor, living among them, a short hundred yards from the field, near a quiet elbow in the creek and near the lonely road, knew the field's enchantment. He loved the field. For over a decade, walking stick in hand, he had cheated time by slipping through the dense undergrowth behind his home and by hurrying past the new concrete bridge, so that he could magically pierce the violet clasp of the field to reflect alone in its peaceful setting.

Entering the field reminded the neighbor of a movie he had seen as a boy, a black-and-white antique about a "secret garden", a garden which came alive in contrasting, vivid technicolor when visited by children. This field was now his adult "secret garden". The seculusion joyfully found there within its portals, seemed so incongruous with the teeming activity nearby. The loud, braking school buses with the happy, home-returning banter of small children as they disembarked, and the congestive string of autos pounding across the new concrete bridge with twice-a-day work and home regularity, appeared epochally distant from the serenity relished at the field. The indifferent avoidance of the field, by so many who lived near it, always perplexed and amazed the neighbor.

Grounding his walking stick and pushing it before him, the neighbor squatted and gingerly passed below the casually maintained barbed wire fence, through his spellbinding discovery window. Slinging aside his daily worries, he exchanged them within the field for a tonic of the mind, a healthful, stirred concoction, passionately drunk in the safe haven of his secret garden.

The fence was weary with neglect. Rotting posts, eaten by time, lounged at all angles in disrepair. Some were loose in the ground like worn teeth with gum disease; others, recent replacements, gleamed new, bright, and straight. All the posts were laced together with interweaving new, gray wire needfully fortifying ancient, rusty strands, which sagged and stooped in retirement.

198

The neighbor would walk about his field in a distinct, predictable fashion. First, he would traverse its long axis, a full mile, then circumnavigate the perimeter entirely near the boundaries, and finally return exactly to his point of entry, an hour later and three miles better off about the heart and lungs. His gait was brisk but unforced. Pauses for poking at gopher holes or watching a bird on the wing were random and unhurried. When inside his beloved field, he had no timetable to serve.

The long hike across to its southern extremity took him directly past the field's most distinguishing feature. There, at almost the epicenter, halfway across, a copse of liveoak trees hugged the rim of the field's solitary pond. The pond was almost perfectly round, a hefty fling of a smooth rock across, and would shrink alarmingly to almost nothingness in the dry season, and then rejuvenate each year to legitimate pond status when the steady, filling rains of summer returned.

The little principality of pond had its monarch. An alligator, not huge but certainly big enough for anxious sun-bathing fowl, cruised this cozy domain like a watchful submarine. On still, clear nights, its croak and honk were audible, ghostly distant, back at the creek and the dusty road.

The sharp definition of pond and its fringe trees, the only trees in the field, was a beacon for pilots of light aircraft. A friend of the neighbor, a pilot who had moved away to the Pacific Northwest, had told of its bullseye clarity from the air and how student pilots and even seasoned ones would swoop down in flight over the pond and trees, practicing their touch-and-go landing exercises.

And the neighbor, also, had viewed his treasured field from high in the sky. Once, returning from a business trip by commercial airliner, he had selected a left side window seat purposely, knowing the arriving flight patterns above his home, and when the plane had begun its long descent, twenty miles from the great city airport to the south, he had easily spotted his field. Although he was not a pilot himself, he had understood the attractive lure of the field from the air.

In his field, the solid crunch of matted grass, garnished with tangled weed, felt secure beneath his step. The grass would thin in winter but then in summer, with greater profusion, pull slightly but not annoyingly against his legs. The field, never mowed, would receive a periodic natural haircut, just in time it seemed, by cows and horses which would appear suddenly, unannounced, at no regular interval, arriving through neglected patches of sagging fence. They would stay for days, indifferent nomads, munching and grazing, ruminating quietly near the pond, in couchant relaxation in some shady spot, and then, without proclamation, they would disappear again for weeks at a time.

Thick, fecund pockets of pasturage, in faint, bowled craters, shallow vanishing ponds, which were soggy and damp, stirred rich and green amid the predominant sea of yellow and tan grass which tossed in any breeze, like the mane of a lion dispatching some bothersome fly. Occasionally, a cactus thorn or a stinging nettle, hidden land mines, would spear through the top of a canvas shoe. Conical ant mounds, self-governing colony cities, which reigned independently like disjointed feudal states, were to be deftly avoided like the cactus and the nettle.

When the neighbor reached the southern flank of the field, the vista stretching before him was repulsive. It was harsh and offensive to the eye. Great, gouged holes, called borrow pits, now filling with greenish, foamy ooze, had been clawed open as acne on the face of the field. Sloping piles of excavated sand, miniature mountain ranges, jutted detestably, barren and stark against the sky, as high as three-story buildings, silent and resolute with their massiveness.

Huge machines, their pulleys, chains, and levers stilled on a Sunday, in a threatening, striking pose, loomed in wait, as giant, petrified insects in eager anticipation of a delectable Monday morning breakfast of earth. On the morrow, they would be awakened. They would then yawn, belch, break wind, and grumble all day with their strained stomach rumble of work.

White, aluminum construction trailers, their windows obscured with dust, sat coldly by, their temporary wooden stairs pushed hurriedly up against battered metal doors. Within them, high-top stools perched precariously by large, slanting drawing boards, cluttered with rolls of blueprint battle plans. In the morning, khaki and denim-clad civilian generals would assemble again to plot their strategy against the field. Their musketry of mortar mix was stacked at the ready, locked away for only a day.

For several years, the development had inched persistently closer to the field. Now, with wave after wave of new streets, the legions of homes were upon the field. The Rubicon had been crossed and there would be no compromise. The field had been invaded and occupied by the unassailable foe. The siege was irreversible; capitulation was imminent.

The neighbor stood by one of the great pits, his neck and face suffused with anger and bitterness. Afloat below him, a single, yellow quart oil can pitched at an angle in the polluted ooze. Undoubtedly, it had been offered to slake the nearby thirst of one of the great machines. Small, triangular openings on its top bobbed close to drowning the can as it slowly moved but it survived for now, atop its inevitable grave. Washed to another watery corner of the great pit, a soppy collection of paper plates, plastic cups and crumpled cigarette wrappers clung together desperately, as shipwrecked men grab for drifting, floating debris.

Turning from the unpleasantness, the neighbor trudged away, beginning with a subdued stumble, his ritualistic survey of the circumference of the field. There, as he began, near the construction command post, a new stripe of a path, in two quickly worn furrows, had been lashed across the broad back of the field. It led away to the creek side. The neighbor followed it.

The path was the new route of a rusty pickup truck which was being used by the development builders to transport their excrement of construction for open dumping across the field at the side farthest from the new homes. The truck could be seen many late evenings, laden with debris, limping and sputtering along the gentle roll no faster than a man could walk. Two young boys always rode atop the load and valiantly fought to keep the construction residue aboard. They never really succeeded. The path was littered each day with scraps of tarpaper and plastic and with greasy, cellophane lunch wrappers.

One evening while walking, the neighbor chanced to meet the truck and its driver. The pleasant, grizzled old man, with a bitten stub of a cold cigar clenched between yellow teeth, stopped to chat with him. From his seat and through the open window, he inquired about the alligator in the pond, which both men had witnessed numerous times. He was a kindly man, who harbored no malice toward the field. He was simply doing his job as asked, oblivious to its avaricious furtherance, as the grabby dream of others.

Like the brooding, stone-faced sentinels of Easter Island, great stacks of emasculated trees slept assembled, evenly spaced for later safe torching. Their pyre of amputated limbs and branches, grotesque and gaunt, was hauntingly frightful, silhouetted against the sky. Nearby, lay piles of trees which had been wholly uprooted. Browning and withering, they were silent in death, discarded for no future use and deprived of a decent burial, their soil homes usurped by concrete driveways, curbings, and sidewalks.

Joyce Kilmer wept.

As the neighbor passed the pond the second time on his rounds, the waterfowl there seemed skittish. Their squawking was loud, shrill, and more frequent than the neighbor had remembered it. The birds lighted, fluttered away aimlessly, lighted again and moved restlessly on their perches. A dragline had paid the pond a visit that week and was welcomed there like an unsympathetic landlord demanding rent that could not be paid. Prints of metal tread leading to the southside of the pond, stamped as dinosaur track, had marauded with their ponderous press of earth. A wide, ugly gash of exposed black muck had been cut as the machine had rumbled and lumbered dim-wittedly to the edge of the pond, like some extinct brute clumsily wasting vegetation beneath it as it searched out a water hole.

Looming rows of termite-treated obelisks, communication poles, had been planted as half-constructed crosses, awaiting the defiant men of Spartacus. Squat, robotic metal relay boxes, Marsian green, hummed with impassive mechanical hearts. Survey stakes, with flapping ribbons of orange and fuchsia, had pricked the sensitive skin of the field. Silver fire hydrants had mushroomed, popping up seemingly overnight, like voracious tropical plants incubating in a rain forest.

The neighbor walked on, approaching the creek side again. There, before him, on the brow of that sector of field, supposedly hidden from the development viewing, lay scattered the worst retina-wrenching spectacle of filth imaginable. There was the depository for the old pickup truck's daily missions, a ground level crypt with only humidity serving as protective lid. The scene was so despicable it was almost fiendishly humorous, as one laughs on with hurting belly long after a slapstick moment ceases to be amusing.

He reflected on the ironic folly before him. As the development had sprouted, the feces from its appetite had to be deposited somewhere. All of it had been carted here. Now, as the development invaded the field, salespeople, marketing homes to prospective buyers, extolling country living at its finest, with waving hands hypnotically clutching maps, glossy brochures, and ready contracts, soon would not be able to hide the cesspool of their own creation.

The construction trash, intended to be removed from repulsive sight, was marching stealthily back to engage the columns of new homes approaching from the other side of the field. Unavoidably, the two characters in the drama would clash at centerstage with the harmony of sun-drenched mayonnaise introduced into a once happy stomach. Utter lunacy was their poorly planned scheme. At some other point, for a second time, and soon, the whole panorama of rubbish would have to be swept beneath earth's rug again. Unable to wheel over the wreckage it had already crudely created, the path of the truck, once across the field, had fanned out into a delta of little tributaries, in an attempt to find new littering locations. The mounds of debris could have built a treehouse or a play fort for practically every eligible Huck Finn boy in America.

Jagged bottles, rusty cans, caulking cylinders of every description. Crumpled sawhorses with broken backs. Galvanized flashing bits, cut in sharp curls. Wood chalks and braces of every length with old nails dripping tetanus. Partially filled drums and pails of mortar mix. Ripped, empty cardboard boxes, bearing brand names, from which hardware, plumbing, and electrical fixtures had been torn. Pink folds of fiberglass insulation and green sewer pipe. Flowered sofas, discarded with protruding sprung coil and tufted tear, sat pew-like, arranged almost neatly, before the altar of man. Half-devoured lunches, putrid in decay. Teeth markings still present in sandwich bread. Faucets, tubing, wire, shingles, carpet remnants with colors running from the rain. An array of useable materials. Fragments, everwhere fragments, like the sentences here describing them. And one powerful, omnipresent theme to the environmentalists - a jettisoned dump with a carbon dated half-life of centuries.

With his shoulders slumped forward in abject defeat, the neighbor drooped along to the great pits again. He stood there a long time, silently, overlooking the nodding voyage of the yellow oil can spotted a half-hour earlier. A breeze had quickened. The can, like a distressed ocean liner, had taken green ooze through its triangular openings. It was tilting more now, rocking with unsteady list, as its balance was altered by the breeze allowing the wash of soupy filth through its open top.

The neighbor stood wearily, anesthetized with resignation, braced upright by his earth-dug walking stick. The stacked houses before him seemed so cold, so impersonal, so detached from care. Craftily disguised with flip-flopped garage designs, shuffled floor plans, subtle variations on trim and color, they really existed as only hasty, cookie-stamped copies of each other. He recalled the view he had witnessed many weekday late afternoons - the ear-splitting cacophany of whining drill and saw, the punishing staccato of hammer and staple gun, the crews of sod bearers flinging browning squares of grass down upon trash-raked sand, the convention of paneled work trucks and double-parked moving vans, the tan barrels and cartons rising in new garages, and the squealing children traversing still framed driveways and fresh sidewalks, exploring new surroundings on unpacked tricycles.

While he moodily suffered, the odyssey of the yellow can was ending. He waited and watched, gnawed by torment. Filling and vanishing, it sank at last without a murmur, without a merciful paean for its trouble. The neighbor turned for home. A distant church bell from a farming hamlet four miles away and the faint, coaxing whistle of a man exercising a hunting dog far across the field, broke the Sunday stillness. The ring of a hammer echoed well back in the development, signaling overtime construction work for some industrious carpenter. There would be more overtime hours on upcoming weekends as Christmas was only a few weeks away and stockings would need filling.

After walking fifty yards toward home, the neighbor, flushed with guilt and embarrassment, turned abruptly off the easy path of the worn truck road he had begun to follow. He had acquiesced to their way, unthinkingly, submissively, in walking their road. He loathed himself for his momentary compliance. He lashed himself privately, scolding the ease with which establishment conformity nets the unwary chancing by, too close to its enslaving snare. The more familiar crunch and tug of natural grass calmed and reassured him.

Hiking home, still within the caress of the field, he passed the ancient grapefruit grove, which was adjacent to the field, outside and to the north, bordering along the dusty road. Unattended for years, the wizened and brittle trees, husbanding themselves, still managed fruit. They were failing so now, neglected, suffocating with weeds. The neighbor reflected. Each year, on the first frosty day of the season, on their traditional walks, he and his father, from the great city a dozen miles away, would stride energetically up the dusty road to pick from the trees. The bounty was scant always but the reward was precious, as the trees had so little to give.

On these fabled cold walks each year, they could be seen, two generations, wrapped in flannel shirts and bulky jackets, joking and laughing, each with walking stick, invigorated by the crisp, biting air. Sometimes, they would be joined on their excursions by the neighbor's son, and then three generations would walk together.

Past the wheezing grapefruit grove, with its skinny, veined limbs of sky-clutching terror, still skirting inside the fence for home, reminded of those times when his son joined them, the neighbor gazed fondly across to the level stretch of the field where he and teen-age boys had taught this son to bat a baseball. It seemed like yesterday, his son crouched awkwardly, desperately balancing a bat as tall as himself, and now this son was grown, a scholarship athlete at a university in another state.

Rich were the memories, and now, fleetingly, only memories they would remain. Years before, a dozen horses had slipped through a break in the puny fence and had led men and boys on a merry roundup through the development where the neighbor lived. This event, a true western scenario, had been labeled the "modern stampede" and its novelty endured fresh in the minds of residents for years. The corraling pickup trucks from the concerned ranch were limited to the roads in the development but the dashing horses had every advantage, knowing no such restriction, as they gamboled over flower beds, through slopping, wet clothes drying on lines, and up and down deadend driveways.

Venturesome cows also had strayed outside the field. Their hoofed clop striking the concrete at night sharply split the still air. And when they stormed through the palmettos and brush, the sound was deafening, like a runaway locomotive plunging down a mountain grade. Once, at the neighbor's home late one night, a cow had foraged meticulously on slender shoots of grass which had survived all along the base of the foundation outside the bedroom window, left behind there, beyond the whirring reach of the lawn mower blade. The cow's rasping, throaty munch over the spare delicacy had entranced the neighbor while he lay quietly, breathlessly, only inches away, separated only by wall and window.

The neighbor paused at his point of entry, this Sunday tryst concluded but he was unable to swiftly depart. He dawdled as one does at a train station when it is almost too late to say goodbye. Fields are people too, he pleaded privately. Haven't they a right to long life and the pursuit of happiness? Was the field consulted and read its rights about its planned execution? Was it awarded rebuttal time? Who, among men would appeal this unilateral death penalty? Were descendents of Seminole Indians gathered by fires at the shore of the pond centuries ago, given a voice for their violated ancestors?

Profoundly sad was the neighbor, sad for those who walk upright and think, who could speak but would not; sad for all those who lay beneath, who once walked and thought and would speak but could not. He was sad for men, like his new acquaintance the trash truck driver, good men who labor, chasing the dreams of others, fashioning through honest effort, innocently and unknowingly, that ill-gotten plunder for those who command their actions.

When will men learn that more can be so much less, and less so much more?

He was sad for himself. Was he really any better than those he accused, than those he assailed for greedy myopia? Was he? Had he not annexed the field to his own exclusive, coveted use, interpreting indifference by others as tantamount to unworthiness for them? Had he not always wished his field vacant, empty, an expansive sward of quiet, baronial oneness with himself?

The neighbor passed his stick before him under the wire, poked for snakes in the grass, and then vulnerably slumped to negotiate his leave. A single barb mockingly tugged and tore

207

at this shirt. Misty and melancholy, he trudged for home, ribboning a long, trailing line of sand behind him, traced by the unconscious droop of his walking stick.

Past the wood thicket, a scant hundred yards away, beyond the dusty road, a powerful auto thundered across the concrete bridge, droned with acceleration, and whisked mightily up the artery of civilization beyond.

ABOUT THE AUTHOR

Born in New York state, Ed L'Heureux grew up in central Florida and has spent his adult life there. He attended schools in Winter Park, Florida, graduated from Stetson University in DeLand, Florida and also studied law at the University of Florida and Stetson University.

Over the past twenty years, he has pursued careers in the securities industry as a stockbroker, in commercial real estate development, and in the field of insurance. Currently, he operates his own insurance agency in central Florida and has done so for the past ten years.

Writing has always been one of his favorite pastimes, with greater emphasis, avocationally, placed with this endeavor in recent years. With a number of magazine feature articles to his credit, THE DOLLAR COLLAR is his first serious collection of short stories in book form. He is currently writing his first novel as well as a new collection of short stories.

He lives in Casselberry, Florida, with his wife, Laura and his two children, Scott and Stacey.

Order Form for THE DOLLAR COLLAR

Please send _____ copies of THE DOLLAR COLLAR to:

Name _____

Address _____

_____

_____

_____

Enclosed is my check for

Price: $6.95 plus $1.00 shipping (Florida residents add 5% sales tax)

Send order forms and   Ed L'Heureux
make checks payable to: P.O. Box 3633
                               Winter Springs, FL 32708